MAN-BEAST

DEBORAH SHELDON

SEVERED PRESS
HOBART TASMANIA

MAN-BEAST

WWW.SEVEREDPRESS.COM

ISBN: 978-1-922551-03-0

For Allen and Harry

1.

Eddie Clark, panting, muscles burning, let the sledgehammer slip from his hands to the earth. Despite the clouds wreathing the sun on this cool October morning in spring, he sweated like a horse. Eddie pushed his hat back on his head and wiped his brow. Setting up the tent was brutal work. Nearly a month with Taylor's Travelling Troupe and he still wasn't used to it. The physical labour, gruelling schedule, lack of sleep. They had packed up from an agricultural show only yesterday, travelled miles during the night to this sheep station and were setting up again, rushing against the clock, to be ready for their first advertised session at three in the afternoon. He contemplated his palms, marvelling that his calluses had blisters. Still, the regular meals had put much-needed meat on his bones, and he liked the feeling of strength in his limbs. Working for the Taylors was much better than life back in Melbourne. Nineteen-year-old Eddie had grown sick of the hustling, sharping and conning, wondering every day if he could afford to eat, find a place to sleep, and whether marks, other dodgers or coppers would bust him up or rob him.

Nearby, Big Stanley stopped knocking in a tent peg and shouldered his sledgehammer. "Had enough already?" he said, grinning. "Come on. A young bloke like you?"

"I don't know how you do it, mate."

"Practice."

The bare-knuckle boxer Big Stanley should have retired a decade ago, back in 1903 when he had been a heavyweight of some distinction in Sydney, even a headliner for a few months, until that brutal KO. Eddie wondered how much longer before the constant punching would scramble the man's brains into mush. That'd be a damn shame. Big Stanley was *smart*. His few years of schooling made him the best educated of them all and he loved reading, so much so that he kept a suitcase full of books. The owner of the boxing troupe, Florence Taylor, always whinged about the suitcase's weight, railing against the waste of petrol. Big Stanley's usual retort was a threat to quit if she didn't like it. That would mean losing not just Big Stanley but also his companion, Hopper, the boxing kangaroo. Hah! That kind of intelligence was precious. As far as Eddie knew, however, the man didn't have any trade other than boxing, and had been making his living that way his whole life.

"Take a smoko if you like," Big Stanley offered. "No worries, I don't mind."

Eddie contemplated the boxer's swollen eye, the bruised knots along his jaw, and said, "Aren't you knackered from the town gig? Sessions all day for three days. Your last bout went the full five rounds, didn't it?"

"Yeah, that drover knew how to duke. Today's only two sessions, mate. Piece of cake."

"Is it always like this?"

"Like what?"

Eddie shrugged. "Busy as a blue-arsed fly."

"Well, towards Christmas is always hectic. But if we stick to the calendar of agricultural shows, we'll make a few spare quid. Enough to have an off-season."

Eddie snorted. "You're joking. Florence and Gilbert Taylor give us an off-season?"

"Usually a week."

"No kidding? Hey, that's not bad. Not bad at all."

Cupping his mouth, Big Stanley yelled, "Jack!"

Jack stepped out from the other side of the tent. He was a tall, thin and wiry boxer; a top earner, in fact, since punters tended to bet against his skinny frame. "Yeah?" he called back.

"Fancy smoko? Eddie's ready for a break."

"Nah, she's apples, mate." Jack hefted his sledgehammer and disappeared behind the bulk of the emerging tent. The sound of his hammering started up again.

Eddie rolled a cigarette and lit one. "What about this place?" he said, gesturing at the wide, open plains of the station. "I don't see outfits setting up a merry-go-round or cattle parade. Where's the knock-'em-downs? The show? There isn't one."

"Still-towning is bloody good money," Big Stanley said. "There's no entertainment in the bush, you see. Isolated people come for the boxing. Stockmen like to bet and they drink like sailors." Big Stanley chuckled. "Ah, don't look so forlorn, little chap. True, there aren't any pubs or whorehouses out here, but think of still-towning as a chance to rest your demons."

"Oi!" came a shout.

Both men looked around.

Mavis was stamping towards them, loosely swinging a sledgehammer by her side in one meaty fist. She was another of Taylor's bare-knuckle boxers, billed 'Mavis the Mauler', a tall, thick-set woman aged somewhere in her fifties. Eddie looked beyond her at the ticket booth and line-up board, which she had erected single-handedly in record time.

"Hey there, Mavis," Big Stanley said. "What's up?"

"What's up is that I'm fucken starving. Where's our lunch?"

Big Stanley pulled a watch from his pocket. "Fair enough, it's after eleven." He nodded at the house and said to Eddie, "Want to check on Pearl? She might need assistance."

Eddie dropped the sledgehammer. "Okay. But only because the stew buckets are heavy."

Big Stanley smiled in such a sage and fatherly way that it brought the blood to Eddie's cheeks. He drew hard on his smoke and set off across the grass towards the single-storey house. Everyone in the troupe had made up their minds: Eddie was young and so was Pearl, the assumption being they would naturally gravitate towards each other. But Pearl was silly and naïve. Eddie, orphaned at an early age, had seen a goddamned lot in his life and shouldn't be dismissed as a kid by anybody.

At the front door, he stamped out his smoke, and prepared to knock. Hesitated. Brushed down his shirt and saw that it was covered in sweat stains. Took off his hat to smooth back his collar-length brown hair, which felt crusty with perspiration and dust. His chin was stubbled; the early start had allowed no time to shave. Ah, fuck it. He went ahead and knocked anyway.

After a few moments, Mrs Reginald Smith opened the door. "Yes?"

"I'm the troupe's mechanic and roustabout, ma'am. I'm here to see if Pearl needs help."

Mrs Smith looked over her shoulder. "Pearl?"

"Yes, ma'am?"

"There's a gentleman here asking if you'd like help."

"In a few minutes, yes, I reckon I would."

Mrs Smith stepped back and opened the door wide for him.

It had been some time since Eddie had been inside a house, especially one as fancy as this. Scrubbed floorboards, a coat rack, framed pictures and paintings on the walls, polished furniture, windows with curtains and clean panes that let in the sunshine... He stalled at the entrance. Clutching his hat, aware of the grime on his hands, he wasn't sure what to do.

"Please, come in," Mrs Smith insisted. "Pearl won't be long. Would you like a drink?"

His dry mouth overcame his shyness. "Yes, ma'am. Plain water will do."

Eddie followed her into the kitchen, a bright and airy room. And there at the stove was Pearl Bennett, a slip of a thing whom the Taylors had picked up in the last town. Slender to the point of malnourished, pale, her wavy blonde hair rippling about narrow shoulders, a pinched mouth that reminded him of a cherry. Pearl Bennett, the most recent addition to the troupe, was a mystery. She kept to herself. Eddie wondered where Dot was hiding, the boisterous Australian terrier forever by Pearl's heel. Mrs Smith would never allow a dog inside. Perhaps Dot was following Hopper around. For some reason, the two animals had bonded. Or maybe Dot was trying to befriend Bluey—

"Oh, hi Eddie," Pearl said. "Good timing. The stew's ready. I just have to pack it."

Mrs Smith offered Eddie a glass of water, which he drained within seconds. Mrs Smith stared at the empty glass and refilled it. This time, Eddie made sure to politely take his time.

Meanwhile, Pearl was ladling the stew into two metal buckets. "I'm so grateful, Mrs Smith," she said as she worked. "I have to make our meals over an open fire and the cooking time is just any old how. A proper stove is such a blessing."

"That's all right, child. And mind, anything you want from my larder, just ask."

"Your vegetable scraps would be good."

Mrs Smith seemed amused. "Scraps?"

"Yes, for Bluey. I think he needs to eat more vegetables."

Mrs Smith looked towards Eddie for confirmation, her brow creasing. "A Yahoo-Devil-Devil needs *vegetables*?"

Pearl turned from the stove. Her hazel eyes, already too big for her face, had widened in surprise. "Why, every creature needs good things to eat," she said. "Even the strange ones. *Especially* the strange ones. They most often miss out, don't you find? Look at snakes. Nobody wants to feed *them* if they can help it."

"Snakes ought to be killed," Mrs Smith said. "As should dangerous creatures entirely."

Pearl pursed her lips and said nothing. She might be silly and naïve, Eddie thought, but she knew when to keep her gob shut. The seconds ticked on, stretched out, got longer and more awkward until Mrs Smith relented, and promised to collect scraps. Pearl thanked her profusely.

Eddie carried the buckets towards the tent. He ambled nice and slow, yet Pearl still had to stride to keep up. At five foot eight, Eddie was tall, sure, but she was *very* short – only some four and a half foot. As usual, she wore a floppy straw hat as shade from the sun.

"You played that old bitch like a fiddle," he said. "Getting her all ashamed of herself."

"Sometimes people need a little nudge to remember the goodness in their heart."

He snorted.

She cut her eyes at him. "What? You don't think people have hearts?"

"Shit, I know they don't. At least, not many do."

"Yeah? Is that so? Well, anyhow."

They walked in silence. He sneaked another look at her. Today she wore her green dress, threadbare and blanched from too many washings. She owned two other dresses – a yellow one with large buttons, and a floral number with a white collar – and they were both just as worn. Once in a Melbourne emporium while shoplifting, Eddie had seen a man buy a half-dozen dresses for his wife. This gesture had made an impression on Eddie. He wished he could buy a dress for Pearl. A mauve one that would highlight the butter-yellow of her hair.

"What did you make for lunch?" he said.

"Irish stew. Potato, onion, carrot. The mutton was thanks to Mrs Smith."

"Gosh, it smells great," he said, hoping Pearl couldn't get a whiff of his own stink.

"That'll be the thyme. Fresh from her garden."

"Thyme?"

"A herb. It goes with mutton."

"Okay," he said.

The conversation ran out. The boxing tent was still some distance away. Eddie wracked his brains, and offered, "Hey, did you know the Smiths get one-quarter of our ticket sales?"

"Oh?" Silence again. Then she said, "I don't know what that means."

"It means if four customers buy tickets, the money from one goes straight to the Smiths."

"That much? How unfair! We do all the work. What do *they* do?"

"Let us use their property."

"So? There's nothing out front except dirt and weeds."

Eddie shrugged. "Florence and Gilbert could either agree to the terms or go jump."

"If that's the case, I'll wrangle as much food out of the old bitch as I can get."

Eddie laughed. After a moment, Pearl began to laugh too. By God, her skin looked as clear and fresh as milk. Had she stayed indoors her whole life? She'd never let on why she'd joined the troupe. Some trouble at home, Eddie supposed. But what kind? A shrill barking started up. Across the paddock, scruffy little Dot raced towards them. Hopper, left behind, stood up on giant haunches and watched, his jaws working a mouthful of grass.

Pearl bent down and scooped Dot into her arms. "How's my baby? Oh, give me a kiss."

The Aussie terrier licked, whimpered, shivered in delight, and wagged her tail.

Eddie appraised the tent, which was now erected, its central flag flying. A wave of unknown and unnamed emotions clamped his chest and pricked his eyes. Big Stanley, Jack and Mavis sat at the trestle table. The Taylors hadn't yet emerged from their caravan.

"Come on!" Mavis bawled hoarsely. "We're starving!"

And nearby under a canvas, chained within a cage on wheels, Bluey wasn't making a sound. Perhaps he was asleep. Or drunk already. Every day upon Florence's instructions, Gilbert plied Bluey with whiskey to make sure no challengers got killed in the boxing tent. Secretly at night, however, Eddie gave Bluey water to drink. The monster seemed appreciative…it was hard to tell. Tom the nightwatchman always looked the other way.

"Irish stew," Pearl announced as Eddie put the buckets on the table. "My mother's recipe."

"Hurry up and serve it then," Mavis said, gesturing with her spoon. "I'm fucken *dying*."

***

The troupe ate lunch, chatting. Everyone sat in their usual places. At one end of the table, opposite each other, were Florence and Gilbert Taylor. Then Pearl and Eddie. Big Stanley and Jack. Finally, Mavis alone, since Tom was sleeping in a motorcar. Pearl had put Tom's lunch aside in the shade and covered it with a tea towel to keep off the flies. Nearby, Hopper fossicked through the grass and Dot followed his every step with interest.

"Would you look at that silly mutt?" Gilbert chuckled. "Seems like she's trying to become a roo herself. Keeps chewing at the grass like Hopper."

"But spits it straight away," Pearl pointed out. "She's not dumb."

"Oh, that little doggie just wants to see what all the fuss is about, I expect," Florence said.

Typically, the Taylors had come to the table gussied up – Florence in a boned-bodice dress that squeezed her middle-aged spread into her bustline, Gilbert in a three-button cutaway frock coat – as if they were dining at a fancy Melbourne restaurant. Florence bitched about Big Stanley's suitcase of books, yet their collection of wardrobe trunks would break a scale.

"Dot!" Pearl called, taking a scrap of mutton from her bowl. "Come here, baby."

The terrier raced over, clambered onto Pearl's lap and eagerly ate the proffered meat.

"Huh, she gulped that quick enough," Gilbert said. "Didn't hardly chew."

"Because it's a tad better than grass, no doubt," Florence sniffed.

"No, because it's a bloody good feed," Mavis said. "Cheers, Pearl."

Florence smiled. "Yes, I have to agree. Irish stew happens to be one of my favourite casseroles and I think you've done a simply marvellous job."

"Too right," Jack added, working his spoon. "This is the best stew I've ever had."

Pearl blushed. "Why, thank you, everyone. I like caring for people with food. If you don't mind me asking, what happened to your last cook?"

"Couldn't stay off the grog," Gilbert said.

"And his food tasted like shit," Mavis added.

Big Stanley sighed and beamed around the table, grinning through lips scabbed from yesterday's bout. "Well, now isn't this a pleasant meal?"

It sure is, Eddie thought. He smiled across at Pearl. This was what being in a family might feel like, he supposed. As if you were welcome somewhere and happened to belong.

A faint, drowsing growl sounded.

The mood broke. Uneasily, everyone glanced towards the covered cage.

Florence dabbed her mouth with a serviette. "Gilbert, fetch Bluey some more booze."

"He's already had a couple of pints."

Florence arched an eyebrow. Gilbert rose from the table with a flounce of his coat tails.

"Christ Almighty." Florence shook her head and her jowls along with it. "The booze I buy for that creature doesn't hardly let me break even."

Which was a lie. Eddie had seen the books. Yeah, he could read. He could figure numbers.

Bluey the Yahoo-Devil-Devil – a beast equivalent to the Sasquatch and Yeti – made the Taylors so much fucking money they didn't know what to do with it. Apart from stick it in the bank. Within a few years, probably as soon as 1915 at this rate, the Taylors would be rich enough to retire. Then what would happen to the boxers? To Eddie, Pearl and Tom? Each worker got fourteen shillings a week, flat. Not enough to sock any of it away.

The boxers deserved a cut of the take. After all, they were the main attraction. The sole reason why punters filled the tent, session after session, laying bets and throwing around pennies, shillings, pound notes. It didn't seem right for the boxers to risk scrambling their brains for 14s a week. No sir. It certainly did not. Eddie Clark wondered about that conundrum, and wondered what he could do about it.

Florence said, "Eddie, run into town after lunch. Tom made some mistakes with inventory and we're short. Pick up whiskey, sawdust, petrol, ice, and as much beer as you can carry."

"Okay."

"Oh, can I come too?" Pearl said. "It's my town, so I can take you straight to every store."

Eddie blushed. Big Stanley and Mavis winked at each other. Jack sniggered.

"Is something funny?" Pearl raised her chin and glared around defiantly. "For your information, I haven't had much chance to ride in a motorcar before, that's all."

"Sure, come along, no worries," Eddie said, but his sudden disappointment pissed him off.

***

Behind the sheep station towards the west, thickening bushland led to a chain of flat-topped mountains smothered in eucalyptus forest, the oil from the trees giving the mountains a foggy, blue haze. To the east towards town, however, the land was mostly flat, covered in scrubby yellow grass, bottlebrush and myrtle bushes, the occasional clutch of gum trees, the lines of farm fences. It was a long drive. Eddie didn't mind in the slightest. Pearl didn't seem to mind either. The Model T Ford bumped along the dirt road, churning dust in its wake. Pearl wore her hat jammed low on her head to stop her hair from blowing around. Eddie figured that if there was any change left out of Florence's note, he might pinch a few pennies for a hair ribbon. What would Florence know?

Pearl was full of questions about the motor car. Prior to joining the troupe a few days ago, she'd never seen one in real life, only on billboards.

"Are those eyes on the front of it?" she was saying. "The two round things on its muzzle?"

"Those round things are lights," he said. "You switch them on to see where you're going in the dark. And it's not a 'muzzle' but a compartment called a bonnet. Inside is the engine."

"What a marvel," she said breathlessly, running her hand over the bench seat. "And you're deciding where it moves?"

"That's right. Look, I'll show you."

Eddie slowed down to avoid tipping and, using exaggerated turns of the wheel, meandered the Model T from one side of the road to the other, while Pearl whooped and held onto her hat. He laughed at her infectious delight.

"Do you want to have a go?" he said.

"Of making it move?" She slapped at his shoulder. "Go on. I can't even steer a horse!"

He smiled. "A motor car and a horse aren't the same kind of thing by a country mile."

"They're not? I wouldn't know. How long have you been mechanic for this outfit?"

"Four weeks or thereabouts."

"And you fix the motorcars when they refuse to start work?"

"Pretty much."

She whistled. "I reckon you're the smartest bloke I've ever met."

"Well, it's not that tricky. There's a handbook in the boot that tells you stuff, like how to straighten an axle, change a wheel, fix a busted spring. And I've got plenty of spare parts." He glanced around, feeling his heart lift at the childlike admiration on her face. "If we've got time after shopping, we can go for a spin around town if you like."

"Oh yes, I'd like that very much."

"The smartest bloke I've ever met is Big Stanley. He went to school for a lot of years."

"Really?"

"Uh huh. He's teaching Mavis and Jack how to read."

Pearl turned on the seat to touch his arm. "Do you think he'd teach me too?"

"Sure. I don't see why not."

She sat back. “Wow. I’ve always wondered what’s inside books. Eddie, if you can read that handbook in the boot, does that mean you can read anything at all?”

“Yeah, I suppose I could. But I don’t know how to teach it like Big Stanley.” He paused. “You never went to school?”

She shook her head.

“How come you joined the troupe?” he asked.

She adjusted her hat, and gazed out the side window for a time. “Mum got herself a new boyfriend and he was starting to take too much interest in me.”

“Sorry to hear that.”

“How come you joined?”

“I got sick of Melbourne,” he said. “Sleeping on the streets, conning, getting beat up.”

They travelled in silence. A flock of white cockatoos, squawking and calling, shot from one side of the sky to the other, rocketing along on large snow-white wings. Up ahead, a half-dozen kangaroos lolloped across the dirt road and back into the scrub. The cool air smelled of mint, menthol and lemon from the surrounding foliage.

“It’s nice out here, isn’t it?” she sighed.

“For sure.”

“You know, I think my luck must have finally changed.”

“Yeah?” Eddie glanced around at her. “Same for me.”

***

The tent was hot, packed with bodies, a swarming and shouting crowd of sweating men and women that weaved drunkenly around an epicentre, a hurricane surrounding the eye which was Mavis and the contender who shuffled in the sawdust, ducking and punching and swinging. Mavis had an open cut above one eyebrow which streamed blood. The contender had lost his front teeth and wobbled on rubber legs. She landed another blow to his mouth. The contender staggered back, got shoved towards the centre by many hands as the whole crowd roared. Punters lifted fists in the air, brandishing notes or coins. Florence and Gilbert moved nimbly amongst them, taking extra bets such as 'double chance by TKO', 'prop bets', and others that Eddie hadn't heard of.

Money changed hands in a flurry. Punters took side bets with each other.

Eddie watched the crowd, a cricket bat held by his side in case of trouble. Big Stanley was doing the same, but with a split lip. As the largest and most formidable looking boxer – tall, heavy-set, with a bald head and cauliflower ears – he was the opening act. Sometimes he'd throw a fight if it meant better money for the house. As an ex-professional, he knew how to make a dive look real. Mavis came next in the line-up, then Jack as 'Black Jack', followed by Hopper as 'Killer Kangaroo' wearing gloves and his feet laced in leather booties to prevent any chance of disembowelling a contender. And the final act, the one that drew the crowds like no other, was Bluey, marketed as 'Man-Beast'.

The contender fell to one knee. A couple of punters dragged him up by his armpits and thrust him back towards Mavis, who belted him with a shot to his floating ribs.

How was Pearl faring?

Eddie caught Big Stanley's eye and got a nod. Then Eddie headed towards the back of the tent. Alongside Jack, Pearl was working the bar: two feed troughs borrowed from the Smiths filled with chipped ice and beer bottles. Like Jack, Pearl wore a pocketed apron for notes and coins, and a bottle opener hung from a chain around her waist.

"Okay?" Eddie mouthed with his eyebrows raised.

She nodded, then gently touched at her hair ribbon and offered a smile. Eddie smiled back. Then she had to take money, give change, open a beer, hand it over. Do the same again. And again, and again. To her credit, she was nearly as fast as Jack.

The crowd roared, the volume making Eddie wince. Mavis must have knocked out the contender. The noise dropped.

"Time to pay or be paid," Florence screeched. "Hurry, hurry, pay or be paid."

"Who's next to take on Mavis the Mauler?" Gilbert boomed. "Who amongst you is man enough to teach this fat old hussy a manner's lesson she'll never forget?"

It was huckster talk, Eddie knew, but that didn't mean he had to like it.

The crowd bellowed in approval. A new contender must have stepped forward.

"Taking bets," Florence yelled. "Hurry, hurry, taking bets. To win. Go the distance. Three rounds over under. Taking bets."

Eddie watched the crowd with its snarling, feverish, savage, urgent faces.

2.

The crowd hushed. Damn, Eddie thought, it's like a Sunday service in here all of a sudden.

"Ladies and gentlemen," Gilbert announced. "Prepare yourselves for a sight unseen by most human eyes. A sight that will stir terror and awe. Kidnapped from the darkest, wildest lands somewhere back of Burke, a monster from a breed that was once the stuff of legends until intrepid explorers discovered it to be flesh and blood. An animal that, if given the chance, will break your skull and suck out your brains…"

Everyone in the crowd was on tenterhooks. Bunched up together, drunk as skunks but no longer boisterous. Gilbert certainly knew how to work them.

"…An animal that we, the owners of Taylors' Travelling Troupe, have educated in the art of boxing. How? Because the Yahoo-Devil-Devil has the small gift of subhuman intellect buried in its brain and can think. Even learn. Is he smarter than *you*, sir? No? You're shaking your head. Well, now what about *you*, good fellow? Could he outfox *you* in a fight? Or *you*, sir? Is anyone brave enough to find out? Tell me, who will fight the Man-Beast? Who will take him on? Who will prove himself a god amongst men?"

Mavis, her eye blackened, opened the tent's side-flap and secured it. Visible were a few bars of a cage. The crowd gasped. Mavis pulled the bolt, swung open the door and stepped back quickly as if frightened, but of course, she knew Bluey was blind drunk.

A growl sounded. An anxious, excited murmuring rippled throughout the tent.

Extending one arm theatrically, Gilbert swept over to the open cage. "Arise, Man-Beast!" he bellowed. "Show your hideous self! Reveal to one and all your devilish visage!"

A clinking of chains. The crowd pressed back.

Eddie had seen Bluey's entrance many times, yet still held his breath, transfixed. First, a giant hand emerged, big enough to sit in, its palm the width of a kitchen chair. The hand had dark grey and wrinkled skin, black fingernails, and bristling ginger hair that grew back from its knuckles. Shrieks sounded from women and men alike. Chains rattled. The stink of unwashed animal fur wafted into the tent.

Then Bluey emerged.

People screamed outright.

He supported himself on his fists like the mountain gorilla, a legendary creature discovered in 1902 just months before the first Yahoo-Devil-Devil was killed by troopers and also confirmed to be real. Bluey ducked his head beneath the tent flap, shuffled his ape-like feet and entered the arena, blinking and swaying, pissed as a newt. About his neck, he wore a metal collar which was attached to a long chain bolted to the cage floor. From the moment of his capture, the collar had never been removed.

Gilbert shouted ecstatically, "I give you…Man-Beast!" and darted away so as not to distract the goggling crowd from the spectacle.

Bluey's height was about nine feet, his weight unknown but Eddie figured at least 500lbs.

Disproportionately large hands and feet. Square head, small ears lying flat against his skull, shoulder muscles the size of watermelons and a chest as big as a wine barrel, the entire body except the feet, breast, hands and face covered in coarse, reddish hair. But the face… No, it wasn't quite the face of a gorilla but almost that of a *man*, a Neanderthal man, with its heavy features and beetling brow. The small, close-set eyes glittered and looked about. There was perception behind those eyes, Eddie felt sure… Perception and intelligence.

"I'll take him on!" a man shouted.

The crowd reacted, turned, parted. And there was Tom the troupe's nightwatchman, bleary from insufficient sleep, the stooge who always got the gambling frenzy started.

Over the top of gasps, exclamations and shouts, Florence yelled, "Bets first, bets, bets!"

Eddie didn't understand the financial side of match-fixing and didn't care. As the crowd surged at Florence and Gilbert, Eddie headed to the back of the tent to check on Pearl. She was behind the bar with Jack, and looked angry with flushed cheeks.

"Poor Bluey can barely stand," she said.

"Aw, don't worry," Eddie said. "He's just blotto."

"I hate this part of the show. Why does he have to be chained up all the time?"

Frowning incredulously, Jack said, "Because otherwise he'd kill every single one of us."

"You don't know that."

Jack snorted. "Yeah, I do. He's a Yahoo-Devil-Devil."

"So? He's got such sad eyes—"

"Listen here, missy," Jack said, gripping her arm. "That monster's not *anything* like Dot or Hopper. It's a killer. It'd eat you as soon as look at you. Understand? Wake up!"

She pulled away. "*Fine*. So, it's a killer." Pouting, she added, "You blokes want a beer?"

"Too right," Jack said, his flash of temper already gone. "Ta, love."

"Have one as well, Pearl," Eddie said. "Nobody will touch the bar for *this* fight."

They watched the performance. The choreography didn't look genuine anymore to Eddie, but the punters bought it. Tom the nightwatchman, an old man of sixty with a serious face, went through his usual pantomime and Bluey responded on cue. Tom jabbed, bobbed, weaved, back-pedalled, feinted, pawed, plodded, landed the occasional blow, while Bluey roared and swept about his giant arms and made it look good. A few times Bluey swatted Tom to the floor, and Tom exaggerated the force, tumbling and sprawling into the feet of the crowd. The tent shook with the volume of cheers, yelps and hollers.

After three minutes, Florence vigorously rang the handbell.

"Time!" Gilbert shrieked, rushing into the middle and shoving Tom aside. "Well done, brave man, you made it to the bell. Here's your winnings!"

He shoved pound note after pound note into Tom's hands, money which Gilbert would retrieve and meticulously count afterwards. Some of these customers were repeats. Didn't any of them recognise Tom from the fights at the agricultural show? Obviously not. And all Tom ever did was change his hat…Now, a genuine punter stepped up to fight. The crowd went wild. Everybody wanted to bet at once. Gilbert and Florence could hardly keep up.

"Look at these suckers," Jack said, chuckling. "Don't they realise the fix is in?"

"Maybe they do, maybe they don't. You've got to admit, the Taylors put on a bloody good show." Eddie took a sip of beer. "How's your chin, Jack? That contender with the moustache bopped you a pretty good one."

"Nah. Hardly felt it."

Pearl said, "I want to take that collar off Bluey. Just once. Let him run around for a bit."

"What?" Jack said. "Are you fair dinkum? Oh, you're as crazy as they come—"

"There's no point in arguing," Eddie said. "The only person with the key to that collar is Florence, and she wouldn't hand it over for all the tea in China."

The crowd roared at fever-pitch, the noise dying down as Gilbert started up his patter.

"The fight must be ready to start," Jack said.

"I reckon so," Eddie agreed.

Pearl didn't say anything. Eddie sneaked a look. Her cheeks were aflame, unshed tears standing in her eyes, little mouth pinched.

***

The evening session played along similar lines to the afternoon session. Now it was after midnight. The full moon shone like a floodlight through the seams and patches of the tent canvas. Eddie, lying awake in the sawdust using his bent arm for a pillow, listened with growing aggravation to the varying snores of Big Stanley, Jack and Mavis. The boxers rattled and wheezed like out-of-tune bagpipes, a demented little orchestra. Eddie checked his pocket watch. It was time to give Bluey a bucket of water, yet Pearl had slipped from the tent some half-hour ago. He was still waiting for her to return and doze off. Giving Bluey anything to drink but whiskey was forbidden – a sackable offence – and Eddie didn't know for absolute certain that Pearl could be trusted.

Minutes kept ticking by. At this rate, Eddie would get hardly any sleep at all.

Where was she? He had assumed at first that Pearl had gone outside for a piss. What was taking her so long? At last, he threw off his thin blanket, leapt up, grabbed a bucket, filled it with melted ice from one of the beer troughs and exited the tent.

The moonlight made everything look monochrome. There was Tom as usual, sitting in one of the motorcars with a loaded Martini-Henry rifle in his hands. Other troupes had tried to steal Bluey; hence, the need for around-the-clock vigilance.

"Where's Pearl?" Eddie whispered.

Tom shrugged. "Not in the tent? I ain't seen her."

The Taylors' caravan was some distance away, the windows dark. Eddie went past the cars and circled the tent towards the other side where Bluey's covered cage was parked—

And froze.

He could hardly believe his eyes.

Perched on one of the cage's wheelhouses sat Pearl, skinny legs crossed, Dot curled peacefully in her lap. Bluey had part of one huge, grey hand sideways through the bars, close enough to grab Pearl. Eddie's heart stopped. Perspiration sprang across his body. Dear God, now Pearl was reaching out her own tiny hand and pressing into those monstrous fingers some kind of object…an apple! A fucking apple! Eddie's blood began to pump again and sing in his ears. In three strides, he was upon her.

"What the fuck are you *doing*?" he hissed, dragging her clear to safety.

She cried out in surprise. Dot and a half-dozen apples tumbled from Pearl's lap. With a yelp, Dot ran beneath the cage.

Recovering her composure, Pearl wrenched from his grasp. "How dare you manhandle me like that!" she said, sotto voce. "You've no right! And you scared my dog!"

"You want to get killed? He'll pull you through the bars of the cage in pieces, you ninny!"

"No, he won't! He's enjoying his supper far too much to do anything of the sort."

"His *supper*?" Eddie gaped at the strewn apples. "Where did you get these?"

"From Mrs Smith's vegie garden. She's got a whole orchard of fruit trees back there."

"You pinched 'em?"

"Yeah," Pearl said, jutting her chin. "So what? You gonna dob me in?" She pointed at the bucket of water he still held. "And what were you gonna do with that? Throw it over him?"

Eddie hesitated. "Not exactly."

"Then what?"

Eddie scratched his cheek, feeling awkward. Bluey, visible through the parted curtain of canvas, was sitting back and watching them argue, meditatively chewing on an apple.

"Well?" Pearl demanded.

"I was going to…"

"Going to what?"

"Give him a drink of water."

"Is that right?" A hint of a smile played across her mouth. "If Florence found out, she'd have your guts for garters. Looks like we're both idiots by your reckoning."

Tom approached at a brisk pace. Once within earshot, he rasped, "You'll wake the whole bloody camp if you keep up this racket."

"But she's out here feeding Bluey *apples*, for God's sake," Eddie complained.

"Yeah, I know."

"You *know*?"

"To be sure," Tom said. "Just as you like to give Bluey water, Mum's the word with me."

Pearl bent down and began picking up the fruit. "See? Tom understands. Tom, how long have you known Bluey?"

"Oh, a year or thereabouts. Ever since we caught him around these parts."

"You caught him *here*?" Pearl said. "At this sheep station?"

"When still-towning last season. A half-mile or so toward them mountains we found him and trapped him." Tom inclined his head at the caravan. "Want to wake them? Then keep the noise down afore the Taylors get wise and dismiss the both of you." He stomped away.

"So, this place is his home," Pearl whispered. "Do you think he would recognise it?"

"He'd have to see it first," Eddie said. "Now stand back and let me give the bludger his drink. I'd like to get *some* sleep tonight, if you don't mind."

He went up to the cage and lifted the bucket. Chain clinking, Bluey shifted closer and pressed his face against the bars, pursing his lips. Slowly, so as not to spill any or choke the monster, Eddie tipped the bucket. The loud swallows sounded like a drain emptying. Did Bluey realise this was water? Or, still drunk, did he assume the bucket held more whiskey?

With a crackling rustle, canvas seams whipped past Eddie's face. He stepped back, startled, as the canvas shrouding the cage pulled away. And there was Pearl on the other side, holding a corner of the canvas in both hands, stepping backwards and hauling with all her might. Eddie clenched his teeth. Oh, for the love of Christ...

The covering came free and fell to the ground. Bluey looked around, blinked, and stood up.

Eddie slammed down the bucket. "What the hell did you do that for?"

"I want him to see his home again. Surely, you can't begrudge a small kindness."

"How are we supposed to put the covering back on without the hooks and pulleys?"

Pearl smiled. "We'll go fetch the hooks and pulleys, that's all."

"From the Taylors' caravan?"

Her face dropped.

Eddie threw up his arms. "Oh, this is great. Terrific. First good job I get, and you ruin it for me. I'm as good as sacked. I may as well become a swagman."

As Bluey began to grunt, they continued to argue in harsh whispers.

"I'm sorry," Pearl was saying. "I only wanted him to see his home. It's been so long—"

"He's an animal, Pearl! One bit of bush would look the exact goddamned same as any other. Now what are we going to do?"

Bluey's piercing howl made them both duck and flinch. Yelping, Dot shot out from beneath the cage and flew into Pearl's arms. Bluey had hold of the bars, his face scrunched in anguish, eyes closed. Dropping his head back, he opened his mouth, showing his long yellow teeth, to let out another loud, agonised howl. Then another. Another.

"What's wrong with him?" Pearl cried.

Goose flesh crawled over Eddie's back. This was a distress call. A *mobbing* call. Desperately, he gathered up the canvas and, stumbling in his haste, tried to cover the side of the cage that faced the mountains.

"Feed him apples!" he yelled. "Distract him with the bloody apples!"

Bluey wailed on. Dot began to bark. Pearl put Dot on the ground and scrambled for the fruit. Tom showed up first, shouting and exclaiming. Then Jack and Big Stanley, followed by Mavis, the boxers sleepy-eyed, puffing and panting, full of questions.

"Shut up!" Eddie yelled. "Cover the cage. He's calling for help. Come on. Hurry!"

Everyone scurried, tried their best, yet without hooks and pulleys they couldn't drag the canvas over the top of the ten-foot-high cage. Bluey kept up his plaintive howls. Being a terrier, Dot joined in. And here was Hopper, surveying the commotion with a puzzled gaze.

"Look Bluey, *apples*," Pearl begged, thrusting the fruit through the cage with both hands like an idiot. Didn't she realise the monster could rip off her arms?

Eddie pulled her clear. "Just lob them," he said. "Don't let him grab hold of you."

"Oh shit, here we go," cried Big Stanley, turning and pointing over his shoulder.

Florence and Gilbert were racing over in leather slippers, their dressing gowns flapping, Florence with her hair set in rags and cold cream on her face, Gilbert carrying a three-pronged harpoon. They both looked mad as hell.

"Holy damnation, who did this?" Florence demanded. "Who took off the cover?"

"Get back all of you," Gilbert demanded, and hoisted the harpoon.

Bluey recoiled and shrank into a corner of his cage, whimpering.

"Oh no, don't hurt him," Pearl implored.

"Shift out the way."

Before Gilbert could thrust the harpoon, Pearl flung herself upon him. He tried to shake her off, but she clung like a limpet until Florence slapped her. Outraged, Eddie shoved at Florence and she fell heavily onto her fat arse. Eddie had a fleeting thought – *Well, there goes my job* – and then the boxers raced over and pulled everyone apart.

"Just put the canvas back on," Pearl cried. "Get the hooks and pulleys—"

"It's no use," Tom said. "Whether you cover the cage or stab the beast half to death, he'll keep a-calling to kin. I'll fetch a motorcar. We'll hitch him up and drive him out of here. It's our only hope."

Bandy legged, Tom hurried off. Bluey started up his howling again, a deep, sonorous resonance that seemed to echo off the mountain range. Eddie had never heard anything like it. The sound raised the hairs on his nape.

"You little bitch, you're *sacked*," Gilbert spat. "Effective immediately. Start walking."

"Too late to sack me, I quit," Pearl sobbed, "I bloody well *quit*."

Florence, getting hauled to her feet by Big Stanley, threw a slipper at Eddie. "And *you* can fuck off and all. Both of you are *vermin*. Absolute pieces of no-good vermin—"

A gunshot rang out.

Startled, everyone faced the house where a lantern swung wildly, getting closer.

"Well, that tears it. Reginald Smith's got his rifle," Gilbert said through teeth.

Pearl quailed. "To shoot Bluey? No, no! He'll be quiet. See? I'll show you." And she raced about, crying, gathering apples.

"He's coming with his shed boss and stockmen," Florence said. "They mean business."

"We'll pay him off," Gilbert said.

"Give him as much as he wants," Florence said. "We can't lose Bluey."

"Shoot that animal dead or I will!" shouted a male voice, presumably that of Mr Smith.

Meanwhile, Bluey kept howling. An engine started up; Tom must be bringing around one of the motorcars. Eddie glanced back and saw, in horror, that Pearl had run to the cage and extended both arms fully between the bars, trying to press apples into Bluey's hands.

"Pearl!" he yelled. "Get back!"

Big Stanley reached Pearl first. Grabbing her about her skinny waist, he yanked her to safety while she kicked and fought. Bluey leapt up, grabbed at his cage and shook it, roaring full-throated and deep-chested, fire in his eyes, rattling the bars with enough force to rock the cage and threaten to tip it. The troupe cowed and stumbled away, awestruck.

Another shot rang out from the approaching Smith crew.

Everyone fell silent, including Bluey.

"Reginald, stop!" Gilbert sang out. "Let's discuss the issue like the reasonable businessmen we both are. Reginald, my good sir, we'll tow our Yahoo-Devil-Devil off your property post haste. There's no need to kill it. The beast brings us a good income."

Reginald Smith put his lantern on the ground. He was stocky, bearded, coarse hands clutching his Martini-Henry. Behind him were six blokes, all armed. Smith addressed Gilbert directly.

"There's a clan of them that lives up in those mountains," Smith said. "They don't bother us; we don't bother them. But your beast is calling them down like a siren. I can't take the risk. Move aside. I'll shoot it dead even if it means shooting you first."

The Model T trundled alongside and stopped, changed gear, and began to reverse.

Gesturing at the car, Gilbert said, "But look, Reginald! We'll be towing our creature now. The danger is as good as past. For your trouble, how about ten pounds?"

"Twenty," Florence interjected, having wiped off the cold cream with her dressing gown.

Smith reloaded his rifle. Pearl hurried to Eddie's side, slipping her hand in his and hiccupping on sobs. Warily, Eddie edged closer to the boxers.

"Twenty pounds for you," Florence continued, "and one pound for each of your men."

"Stand out of the way," Smith said, lifting his rifle.

"Thirty for you and two pounds per man," Gilbert said. "Three pounds, gentlemen! Five!"

The stockmen hesitated, glancing around at each other. Smith caught the change in mood and became incensed.

"I'm head of this station," he said, "and you lackeys follow *my* orders."

Tom braked, jumped from the car, and hobbled to the cage to hitch it on the tow bar. As if understanding that he would be taken away, Bluey howled, long and plaintive.

"So, it's decided," Florence said, forcing a laugh, fluttering about and touching at the rags in her hair. "Thirty and five apiece. I'll get the cash box. It's always best to settle up straight away, in my opinion. Then we'll have a drink. Whiskey? We have beer if your men prefer—"

From the distance came roars.

Low-pitched and loud, like those of tigers and lions from a zoo.

Raucous. Echoing from the mountain ranges.

Then the rustling, breaking, snapping sounds of branches and foliage getting trampled.

Cockatoos, galahs, kookaburras and other birds lifted from the bush in terrified flight and fled screeching across the night sky. Despite the moon casting the world in grey, Eddie saw the blanching of Smith, his men, the troupe. Pearl's hand, clasped within Eddie's own, trembled. In contrast, Bluey panted with joy, hopped in excitement, threw back his head and bellowed high and clear with exaltation. The answering clamour rolled down from the mountains. The splintering of trees sounded like an avalanche tearing through the bush.

"Let's get out of here!" Gilbert yelled.

"No time," Smith said. "They're almost upon us. Grab your weapons. Take position!"

The Smith crew ran to take cover behind the tent, cars, caravan, each man kneeling to keep himself steady and sighting along his rifle towards the bushland to the west.

The shaking of treetops revealed the passage of giant animals coming straight at them at speed. The members of the troupe turned in circles and gaped at each other in panic.

"What do we do?" Pearl cried.

"Get in the motorcars and go!" Eddie shouted.

"Good idea," Big Stanley said, rounding up Mavis and Jack, ushering them to the motorcar that Tom had brought around. "Wait, I've got to get Hopper. Where is he? Hopper!"

"It's just a *kangaroo*!" Florence threw herself into the passenger seat. "Gilbert, hurry!"

"I'm not leaving Hopper," Big Stanley said, and lumbered off to search.

"And I'm not leaving Big Stanley," Mavis said, following him.

Jack looked torn. "Kids, jump in the car with the Taylors," he urged, shooing frantically at Eddie and Pearl. "We'll take one of the others." And then he was gone too.

Pearl scooped up Dot. Eddie gripped Pearl's arm and ran towards the revving Model T.

But Gilbert, having vaulted into the driver's seat, began driving away pell-mell with his wife. Tom limped after them a few yards, following their rooster tail of dust.

"Bloody cowards!" he bellowed. "May you scratch a beggarman's back one day!"

"What does that mean?" Pearl gasped.

"Dunno, I'm not Irish. There!" Eddie pointed at the motorcar with the trailer that stowed the tent and other belongings. "Come on, Tom! Let's ditch."

"Boy, I've got a rifle," Tom called from the road. "There's also a gun in my pack. I'll—"

Ear-splitting roars made Eddie and Pearl spin around.

Three Yahoo-Devil-Devils barrelled out of the bushland, charging and baying, running on feet and knuckles across the cleared land of the station. They shook their heads, bared their teeth, jaws slavering. Each roar vibrated through Eddie's entire body, shaking him to the bone marrow, rooting him to the spot in shock. His first coherent realisation was: *These monsters are fucking huge*. While Bluey was nine feet tall, these three were twelve feet and more, legs and arms as thick as tree-trunks, hair brown or black instead of ginger like Bluey. Eddie's blood ran cold. Momentarily, he felt faint. Bluey was a *juvenile*. Perhaps even a *child* – if true, the wrath of these Yahoo-Devil-Devils would know no bounds.

3.

Gunshots rang out, jolting Eddie from his stupor. Smith and his men had fired their rifles in defence. Not that it made any difference. Undeterred, the Yahoo-Devil-Devils were closing the distance in a galloping gait, the pounding of their feet and knuckles shaking the earth. Now, taking the beeline to a motorcar meant running *towards* the monsters. Screw that.

"Come on," Eddie urged.

Dragging Pearl by the hand, they rushed into the tent through the gap used for Bluey's access. Dot mewled in the crook of Pearl's arm.

"Where are we going?" Pearl said.

"The long way 'round."

Flinching from the deafening roars and gunshots, they sprinted over the sawdust, burst through the front entrance and headed along the side of the tent to where the remaining motorcars were parked: the one with the trailer for the tent and, behind that, the motorcar hitched to the Taylors' caravan. Eddie and Pearl peeked out, the ruckus sounding on and on.

"All right, make for the motorcar with the trailer," he said.

"What about everyone else?"

"We'll pick 'em up on the way. The coast is clear. Go!"

They went to run. A great beast with its black hair turning silver lumbered to the motorcar. Eddie and Pearl ducked back. The beast hadn't seen them as its anger seemed focused on the vehicle. Raising both arms high above its head, it brought down huge fists and crumpled the roof of the Model T right down into its bench seats, buckling the chassis so that the front wheels reared high off the ground. Another pummelling flattened the bonnet. Incensed, the silver-haired beast next picked up the trailer, twisted it free and hurled it one-handed. Bags, crates and supplies scattered as the trailer sailed through the air. It landed some twenty feet away and bounced, a broken ruin.

Good God, Eddie thought, the unbelievable *power* of this animal.

The silver Yahoo-Devil-Devil beat at its chest – *thock-thock-thock* – an unexpectedly hollow and wooden sound, unlike anything Eddie had ever heard before. Such strangeness terrified him more than the roars, more than the strewn wreckage of motorcar and trailer—

Something tugged at his hand.

It was Pearl, still holding on.

"What are you waiting for?" she snapped, white-faced. "Head back the other way."

She dragged Eddie in her wake and he stumbled after her, shell-shocked. They passed the entrance to the tent and, momentarily, he had the craziest desire to mosey inside, curl up in the sawdust under his blanket and just go to sleep, to opt out of this living nightmare. He couldn't stomach the gunfire, the roars, the screaming of men—

Oh Jesus.

The screaming of men.

Pearl pulled up short at the side of the tent. Eddie stopped too.

Reginald Smith was on the ground, bucking and flailing, trying to sit up, his legs mashed into unnatural shapes. Nearby, a body covered in blood lay still. A Yahoo-Devil-Devil with greying hair on its jaws swept a long arm through the remainder of Smith's team, strewing them about. Hoisting one man in its enormous hand, the monster bit off the man's head and spat it like a peach pit. Blood fountained from the man's neck and his limbs jerked from the firing of severed nerves. One more bite – this time into the torso – and the corpse lost its animation. The monster lost its interest, and tossed the mangled corpse aside.

Pearl fell back, retching. Trembling hard enough to lose his own balance, Eddie pulled the little girl to her feet. Somehow, Pearl still had hold of Dot. The terrier seemed limp and unconscious. Eddie had to protect them both. But what to do?

"Let's hide," he said.

Pearl's eyes opened and blinked. "Where? *Where?*"

He looked about, and landed upon an idea. "The house."

"Too far away."

Eddie shouted in fear and surprise as something loomed in his vision.

"It's only me," Big Stanley said. "You both okay?" His face ran with blood from a deep scalp wound, his chin dripping, undershirt soaked red to the waistband of his shorts. "Listen," he continued, "we've got a plan."

Tom appeared from behind him. "Mavis, Jack and Hopper are at the front gate. With the tent in the way, we can escape on foot without them seeing us, maybe get a good lead."

"Along the road?" Pearl said. "You think we can outrun them all the way into *town*?"

"It's daft, I know, but it's all we can think of."

Eddie found his voice. "How about the house? We'd have to dash like billy-o."

"Impossible—" Big Stanley began just as the tent lifted up.

The iron pegs ripped from the ground. In flight, one of them caught Big Stanley across the arm and opened his shoulder to the bone. He dropped. The canvas tent balled up and was swept aside. A Yahoo-Devil-Devil with a wrinkled face and one eye leaned over and bellowed, its hot breath fanning them. Pearl screamed.

A grey hand reached out and plucked up Tom.

In horror, Eddie watched as the old Irishman was raised to the monster's drooling maw. The yellowed fangs closed delicately about the top of Tom's head. Simian lips puckered like a kiss. Eddie lost his breath. The teeth bore down. The popping sound was crisp, gristly, like the snap of bacon on the griddle. Eddie squeezed his eyes shut. He became aware of his own tears, of gagging, the whirl of the world as it spun fast and crazy—

Then a hard, stinging slap to his cheek.

Shocked, he opened his eyes. Pearl's face looked fierce, hectic, pale.

"Help Big Stanley!" she demanded.

Ashamed, Eddie hurried to Big Stanley's side and said, "Give me your hand."

The boxer shook his bloodied head, panting and wincing. "You go, I'll catch up."

The Yahoo-Devil-Devil, preoccupied with chewing at Tom's corpse, was already down to the man's legs. No time to argue. Eddie and Pearl ran towards the gates. Mavis, Jack and Hopper, as if in a relay race, started running too. Jack kept turning around to wave them on.

Faster, *faster*.

Just yesterday, Eddie had driven that road with Pearl to get beer, petrol, sawdust and whiskey. "*You know, I think my luck must have finally changed...*" On the way back from town, she'd held the hair ribbon he'd bought for her at the haberdashery. A mauve ribbon to complement the butter-yellow of her hair. She'd held the ribbon with reverence, as if it were an article of great monetary value, a diamond tiara. None of that seemed real now. Yesterday felt like a fever dream from a long time ago. The monsters would soon be on their heels. Eddie decided not to look back. He would run and run and run, and not look back. Instead, he would allow Death to catch him unawares.

Until shrill, metallic wrenching noises caught his attention, forcing him to look.

Both he and Pearl stopped, and spun around.

The Yahoo-Devil-Devils were rending Bluey's cage. The bars popped apart. Bluey leapt free. The monsters mobbed him at once, hugging, hooting, making excitable *ha-ha-ha* noises as if they were laughing. Bluey squealed and kissed at their cheeks. Oh, this was a joyous reunion all right, no doubt about it, the body language undeniable. Perhaps one of these giant monsters was even Bluey's father. His father!

A shadow of memory, a flash of loss... Despite his terror, Eddie's mouth wobbled into a triumphant smile. No more organ-grinder-monkey routine for *you*, he thought. No more whiskey, no lonely half-life trapped within a cage. Just freedom, family, friends—

The silver monster gripped Bluey's collar in both hands and broke it open. The collar fell with a clink of chains. Rolling his head, Bluey rubbed at his throat just like a man at home on a Sunday after loosening the tie he'd worn to church.

The other Yahoo-Devil-Devils, anger spent, started to dawdle towards the mountains. Eddie's shoulders sagged in relief. They were leaving! The danger had passed. But then Bluey glanced back, noticed the fleeing troupe, and took after them at a gallop.

Adrenaline nearly stopped Eddie's heart. "Run!" he screamed.

Mavis and Jack saw Bluey's approach and redoubled their efforts. Hopper veered into the scrub. The terrier squirmed from Pearl's grip and dashed after the roo.

"Dot!" Pearl cried in anguish, and went to pull away.

Eddie refused to release her hand. "She'll be safer with Hopper," he said. "Come on!"

He kept bolting, hauling Pearl in his wake, straining to catch Mavis and Jack as if safety lay in numbers. His feet thudded the dirt. He hadn't sprinted this hard since a gang with knives had chased him through Melbourne laneways, his fear and a split lip tasting metallic. He'd always been a fast runner. For a moment, he had an absurd image of Pearl fluttering behind him like a streamer, both her legs off the ground. Then fresh sweat sprang to his armpits and the skin tightened on his buttocks because he could hear Bluey getting nearer, the trot of simian feet and knuckles getting louder.

Death had arrived.

How unfair. Eddie was only nineteen years old. Little Pearl even younger.

Please God, let it be quick.

As Bluey reached his peripheral vision, Eddie braced for the worst. The monster overtook them instead. Perhaps Bluey was running away too? Joining them? Eddie imagined a Melbourne flophouse, a room shared with Bluey, the two of them scouring the newspapers and seeking jobs together, Bluey with a trilby perched on top of his huge head—

And then Bluey circled around, snatched up Pearl in one hand, and headed back along the dirt road. Pearl's terrified scream was long, loud and piercing. Eddie skidded to a halt. Flushed with renewed energy and desperation, he sprinted flat out in pursuit, legs burning, heart bursting. The monster was too fast. Pearl's crying voice was already fading into the distance. Holy Christ, the thought of Bluey crushing her to pieces or biting off her head made Eddie sick with terror and fury. But what could he do?

Shoot to kill the bastard.

Loaded rifles must be strewn over the ground. Eddie dashed through the Smiths' gate. Bluey had caught up to the other Yahoo-Devil-Devils on the far side of the yard. Strolling together, excited, gibbering in their strange tongue, the monsters were making for the bush. As he ran, Eddie scanned the yard's wreckage, destruction and death, searching for a weapon. Injured stockmen groaned and wept. Had Bluey already killed Pearl? Good God, Eddie couldn't bear the thought. If he spotted her bloodied, severed head on the ground, he might—

There! A rifle!

Spilling to his knees, Eddie grabbed the weapon, struggled to his feet, ran on, checked the breech, saw that it was loaded. If he could just shoot into Bluey's back…

Bluey was walking one-handed, lopsided, as if he held in his other paw—

"Pearl!" Eddie shouted, stripping his throat raw. "*Pearl!*"

Her reply was a long scream. *She was still alive.* The Yahoo-Devil-Devils stepped over the fence into the bush. Eddie charged faster, pushed harder. The cleared land of the Smiths' yard went on and on. Finally, Eddie reached the fence. Stumbled and stopped. Wheezing, he peered into the bush, through the ironbark and wattle, past the shrubs and grasses.

The Yahoo-Devil-Devils were gone.

And with them: Pearl.

Eddie must have passed out. Someone turned him over. He found himself blinking at a night sky, puzzled, the cold stars and planets wheeling overhead.

"Mum?" Eddie murmured, groggy.

"Yeah, not quite," Mavis said. "Wake up, mate. We're off to rescue Pearl."

Galvanised, he sat up. Jack squatted nearby and patted at his shoulder.

"Where's Big Stanley?" Eddie said, looking around.

Mavis shook her head, mouth set tight and grim. "Dunno. We can't find him."

***

Pearl's head lolled. She was snoozing on a train. A rickety, rocking old train rattling along wooden tracks, jostling her in her seat. Grandma had once taken her on such a trip to visit distant relatives in Melbourne. Pearl remembered the smell of coal smoke, the taste of boiled lemon-drop lollies, the sight of weatherboard houses whisking by on either side of the track with groups of excited children waving. *Chug-chug-chug* sounded the train's engine.

Dazed, she looked about through sleepy eyelids. The train wasn't moving through a city but through the bush at night. Gum trees, bottlebrush, banksia bushes, wattle… The moonlit landscape hurried by in shades of grey. Exhausted, she closed her eyes. Her cheek rubbed against something coarse, a kind of material as smelly as a wet dog, which reminded her of Dot and woke her again in an instant. Where was Dot? And what kind of train had seats covered in…was this *hair*?

Startled, she came fully to her senses.

She was cradled against ginger hair and stinking body heat. The rocking was the gait of Bluey as he walked uphill, the *chug-chug-chug* the huffing and panting of his breath. She looked up and saw his jutting, hairy chin. Looked down, and it was as if she were sitting in a chair: her calves hung freely, but her thighs were gripped in his hand, her reclining figure pressed against his body by his arm. Bluey was carrying her in much the same way as she herself carried Dot.

Shrieking, Pearl sat up and tried to kick loose.

Bluey glanced at her. His lips rippled into something like a smile. With the forefinger of his other hand, he tickled her lightly under the jaw. Then, ignoring her, he continued his trek through the bush – with the three other Yahoo-Devil-Devils that had ripped through the sheep station like a cyclone, killing and maiming. The memory made Pearl feel faint. They trekked single file, Bluey bringing up the rear, plucking leaves as they went along and chewing them.

And what was that noise?

Why, these animals were *singing.* At least, their noises reminded her of singing. The tuneful humming suggested contentment or satisfaction – even happiness – and while they weren't singing the same 'song', their humming noises seemed to complement each other. Pearl found herself laughing silently, hysterically, even as tears streamed down her face. Kidnapped by singing Yahoo-Devil-Devils. What next? A synchronised dance routine by koalas? It would be funny if it weren't so…weren't so…

Her racing heart seemed to trip over itself and her lungs couldn't pull enough air. The corners of her vision went black. After that, the world disappeared.

***

Eddie checked the motorcar. Mostly full tank of petrol, two more fuel cans, three rifles, boxes of ammunition. In his waistband, he had Tom's six-shooter revolver, loaded, the spare bullets loose in his pockets. Oh God, poor Tom… *Don't think about what happened.* Mavis and Jack were hurriedly packing the car with other supplies. Water. Tinned food. Whiskey. Blankets. Christ only knew how long this rescue mission might take. Bandages, iodine—

The thundering of hooves drew their attention. They turned towards the homestead where four armed men on horseback, hats pulled down low, were galloping from the nearby stables. The riders weaved around debris, the dead and wounded. In their wake cantered Mrs Reginald Smith on a fat little pony which was clearly a pet accustomed to leisurely four-beat walks along easy trails. Mrs Smith's hair was loose from its bun and streaming wildly about her shoulders.

The four men loped their horses towards the back fence and cleared it with a jump. Within moments, the bush swallowed them up. Instead of following them, however, Mrs Smith approached the motorcar, reining in her fat hobby-horse just a few feet away.

God, the poor woman.

Even in his terror for Pearl, Eddie felt deep sympathy for Mrs Smith, with her grief-stricken eyes puffed and reddened. She wore an oilskin coat half-buttoned over a nightgown teamed with leather boots. Eddie recalled Reginald Smith and his mashed legs, and looked around for him.

"Those demon beasts have stolen my husband," Mrs Smith said as if in answer, her voice nasal and thick with tears. "One of our shearers too. I've sent four of our men into Woop Woop to mount a rescue."

"And we'll be straight behind them," Jack said. "They stole one of ours: the cook."

The pony shied and fought the bit. Mrs Smith yanked hard at the reins and said, "I'm off to get a posse together from town."

"What about your injured men?" Eddie said. "There's two of them, at least."

"Our wool-table girls are to care for them until I can get a doctor out of bed."

Mavis said, "How will your posse know where to go? It's a bloody big mountain range."

Mrs Smith's eyes flashed. "By following the trail of destruction through the bush, of course. Gads, woman! Are you an imbecile?" The mistress of the sheep station pulled the reins, dug her spurs into the pony's flanks, and headed towards the gates at a stumping trot.

"Strewth," Mavis said. "What a bitch."

"Hey, she's under a lot of strain," Eddie said.

Mavis skewed a wet, angry eye at him. "Aren't we all?"

"Okay, let's go," Jack said, leaping into the front passenger seat of the Model T, while Mavis wedged herself into the back.

Neither of them could drive. If something should happen to Eddie out there in the wilderness, could they figure out between them how to work the motorcar? The handbook was in the boot, yet they were still learning to read from Big Stanley. *Don't borrow trouble*, Eddie reminded himself, a saying his mother used to espouse, and he pushed the troubling thought aside. He double- and triple-checked the position of engine levers before winding the hand crank – Jesus, imagine accidentally running over himself at a time like this – and once the engine started, hopped behind the steering wheel and rode across the yard.

The back fence had a broken section wide enough to accommodate the car. He swung a U-turn, braked, and pressed the reverse pedal.

"What the hell are you doing?" Mavis cried. "Drive on! Stop wasting time."

Annoyed, he had to remind himself that Mavis, like most country Australians, had no more idea of motorcars than submarines or telephones. "The reverse gear is strongest," he said. "It'll be faster going backwards, trust me." He put one arm over the seat, and looked out the rear window.

"Wait!" Jack cried.

Eddie stamped the brake. "Christ, now what?"

Jack opened his door. High-pitched barking preceded the leap of Dot into Jack's hands. He gathered the terrier into his lap and slammed the door shut.

“We’re taking the dog?” Eddie said. “Why not Hopper? We could strap him to the roof.”

“Calm down, mate,” Jack said. “Dot can follow her nose and help us find Pearl.”

Eddie stood on the pedal and powered the car boot-first into the bush. Dot struggled free from Jack’s hands to stand in the back seat and stare out the rear window. Eddie felt a rush of renewed hope: if anyone could track Pearl, it was this devoted terrier.

The car’s engine whined. The wheels trundled. Unseen animals skittered out of the way. Eddie, weaving around trees and shrubs, imagined shooting Bluey right between the eyes. Unless the four horsemen from the Smith station got to him first. Those horses would be well used to mountain travel, would be dashing up the steep and stony hills at speed, their hooves unerring. Eddie cursed his slow and clumsy motorcar until he remembered its one important advantage: this ‘mechanical horse’ was unable to feel fear.

***

Dawn. The cluck of wattlebirds. Warble of magpies. Sunshine glowing a soft pink across her closed eyelids. Pearl knew well the sounds and sights of early morning. At first light, it was her job to start the washing for the day while her mother heated the iron and got to work on yesterday’s laundry, now bone-dry on the racks and lines, ready to be pressed in time for returning customers in the afternoon. Pearl fetched the bucket of boiling water from the stove and took it to the tub outside to begin the soaking. She grated the soap, grabbed the washboard, the dolly stick. Birds kept up their gentle songs. Yet their songs were deep and rumbling, and resembled a weird kind of humming—

“Pearl. Are you awake? Pearl!”

Was that a voice? She lifted her head and found herself draped along Bluey's thigh. She sat up with a yelp. Gently, Bluey took her in hand before she could flee. She struggled for a moment before yielding, powerless. She took in her surroundings. A clearing amongst trees... And Yahoo-Devil-Devils seemingly *everywhere*; some sitting, others lounging, some lazily plucking at branches and stripping leaves with their mobile lips, chewing and humming. Pearl began to hyperventilate, her vision dimming.

"Pearl. Can you hear me? *Pearl!*"

She steeled herself. "Big Stanley, is that you?"

"Over here."

She craned her neck. There, leaning against a gum tree, was the Yahoo-Devil-Devil with the one eye – its other socket a twist of gnarled, scarred flesh – and on the leaf litter by its hand lay Big Stanley, supine. Painted head-to-toe in dried blood from his scalp wound and lacerated shoulder, he looked like an animated corpse, and Pearl recoiled in revulsion and terror. In the next moment, she scolded herself for such a hateful reaction. Big Stanley was badly wounded, deserving of care and compassion. Even as she watched, One-Eye flicked idly at Big Stanley with a forefinger, moving the injured man's limbs around as if the man were a senseless toy.

"Oh my God," she cried. "Can you stand up?"

"He won't let me," Big Stanley said.

"But could you if you wanted to?"

"Probably not."

Pearl teared up in fear and frustration. "Oh, why did they take us?"

"That's got me beat. They have Reginald Smith and one of his men too."

"Which makes four," she said. "One each. Do you think we're…battle souvenirs?"

"You tell me and we'll both know."

She looked around. "I don't see the others. Where are they?"

With effort, Big Stanley lifted an arm to point. One-Eye responded by daintily taking Big Stanley's wrist between forefinger and thumb, and waggling the arm full-length so that the boxer's whole body shook.

Big Stanley groaned. "The bastard's a cat and I'm his injured mouse."

"Oh, don't say that—"

"Soon he'll get fed up and kill me outright."

"No, he won't!" Pearl said. "We'll get away first."

"How?"

"By outsmarting them. We'll think of something, sure enough—"

Suddenly, Bluey lifted Pearl close to his face and gazed upon her. His mouth issued a sour breath. Pearl shrank from those long, yellow teeth. *Was he about to eat her?* She kicked for a few moments then gave up. No use praying for deliverance. If God existed, well, he was clearly indifferent. While Grandma had believed fervently in religion, the same fire had never quite taken in Pearl's breast, and heaven might not exist either. She closed her eyes and prepared for death.

4.

And kept waiting.

Pearl opened her eyes. Saw Bluey puckering his lips. Gasping, she struggled anew in his grasp. The pursed simian lips descended. Instead of biting, however, the mouth landed a kiss on her crown. The shock of still being alive voided Pearl's bladder.

Bluey put her down, allowing her to rest again on his thigh. Sobbing, she gazed about.

On the other side of the clearing, the giant Yahoo-Devil-Devil with the silver hair reclined on its back, dangling a limp Reginald Smith by his arms this way and that like a grotesque nursery mobile. The poor man's legs were corkscrewed and bent at wrong angles.

Quickly, Pearl looked away. Even as she felt the blood draining from her face, she was determined not to faint. Making fists, she scanned the clearing for Smith's worker.

Stripping branches from a banksia and arranging them as if into a nest was a stubby little Yahoo-Devil-Devil with bright orange hair the colour of marmalade. Why, he couldn't be more than three feet tall! And nearby, grooming at her own hairy forearm with fingers and lips was clearly the creature's mother, for Mama had a drooping chest with long nipples, freakishly reminiscent of breasts, and was keeping a watchful eye on the titchy one.

Next to Mama was a female nursing a baby. The female had a relatively unlined face, hair the brown of a newly-minted copper farthing, while the baby's hair was strawberry-blonde...

Size and hair colour denoted age, Pearl deduced, and the chest denoted sex.

Therefore, the clan had three adult males: Silver, One-Eye and the Yahoo-Devil-Devil with greying hair along its jawline which she decided to call Mutton Chop. Silver must be the eldest and perhaps the leader, as he was certainly the largest.

Then Pearl noticed Mutton Chop's feet and could hardly believe her eyes. The toes of both feet were interlaced, much like a person would interlace their fingers, and she had never before seen a pair of feet so queerly resemble a pair of human hands. She was about to remark upon this oddity to Big Stanley when she realised that those clasped feet held the crumpled body of a man, folded in half the wrong way, with the back of his head pressed into the back of his knees.

Nauseated, her palm clapped to her mouth. She wanted to scream but, no, she had to control herself. Stop allowing emotions to get the better of her. Devise a plan, a way to escape. It was her duty. After all, this catastrophe had been *her fault*. Fresh agonies of guilt and remorse lashed at her so cruelly, she feared she would go mad. If only she hadn't removed the cover from Bluey's cage… No, stop. She had to think of a plan to get Big Stanley out of here. But she *couldn't* think. Her mind raced, full of self-recriminations and countless panicked thoughts that darted blindly here and there.

She was lifted again in Bluey's paw and cried out. He brought her level to his face. Dear God, what was he going to do now? Bite her? Throw her? Pearl's heart thudded.

He presented her with a twig of eucalyptus.

What could it mean? As she stared at the offering, he grunted, waved it at her, thrust it closer. Uncertainly, she took it from him. Bluey watched as if expecting her to *do* something with the twig. He grunted again. Was he getting angry?

"I don't understand," she whispered helplessly, and tried to return the twig.

Bluey took it, delicately bit off a leaf and chewed. Then he handed the twig back.

"I reckon he's trying to give you breakfast," Big Stanley said.

"Has One-Eye tried to feed you too?"

"Not a chance. Cats don't bother to feed mice."

"Don't talk that way," she said. "Oh, what should I do with this blasted twig?"

"Make believe that you're eating it."

She put a leaf to her mouth and moved her lips. Bluey made a *ha-ha-ha* sound as if pleased. With his free hand, he stripped branches from a nearby banksia and devoured the red flower-heads with plenty of humming and lip-smacking.

"Big Stanley?" she said. "It's just the two of us. Mr Smith and his worker are dead. As soon as Bluey puts me down, let's try to make a run for it."

"Not me. I'm too weak."

"Too *weak*? What rot! You're a powerhouse. I've seen you keep going, fight after fight, when any other man on earth would have called it quits. Why, you could run the whole day long if you put your mind to it."

"I'm bled half to death."

"Then I'll help. You can lean on me."

"On you?" Big Stanley managed a chuckle. "Child, a stiff breeze would knock you over."

Stung, she looked about the clearing, determined to find something – anything – that could aid their escape. And there, broken off and lying near a clutch of stringybark trees, was a long and relatively straight branch with a crook at one end. It might serve as a crutch if Big Stanley put the crook under his armpit. And those stringybarks were close together, perhaps three feet or so between trunks, too narrow for a Yahoo-Devil-Devil to pass between.

Excitement tingled at her fingertips. Once Bluey put her down, she could run with Big Stanley towards those stringybarks. She would hand him the branch to lean on, drape his other arm across her shoulders, and they could slip between the trunks and dash like hell into the scrub before the beasts even knew what had happened. There were more than enough shrubs to hide beneath, enough big gums to hide behind. Unless Yahoo-Devil-Devils had a good sense of smell – and Pearl chose not to consider that as a factor – she and Big Stanley could take cover whenever necessary. Surely, the Yahoo-Devil-Devils would lose interest after a while and give up the chase?

Pearl's heart flittered in elation. Why, they were as good as free!

All they had to do was head in the right direction. The Smiths' station was east of here… She was looking into the lightening sky through the crown of tall trees and wondering if she could tell which direction the sun was rising, when Mutton Chop grunted and sat up straight. Pearl frowned.

What was the beast doing?

Mutton Chop released the man from between his clasped feet, and used a forefinger and thumb to lift him by his head. The broken corpse unfolded like a pamphlet. What a sickening, ghastly sight… But then the man *moaned.*

Pearl's hands flew to her mouth. He was alive! Somehow, that poor soul was still alive!

"You're not alone," she called, voice trembling. "Mister, there's me and another bloke here with you. We'll get you out of this somehow and escape. Take courage."

How could she support both Big Stanley and the man, whose back was clearly broken? No matter, she would find a way. She simply *had* to find a way.

Mutton Chop made a sharp barking sound. The other Yahoo-Devil-Devils stopped to pay attention. Pearl held her breath. Mutton Chop waved the man about, as if showing him to the clan, and then began to tug and tear the clothes from his body, peeling him naked like an orange while the man puled and wept.

"Oh God, what's happening?" Pearl cried.

"Don't look," Big Stanley said, as if he knew what was coming. "Keep your eyes shut."

Stripped, the man appeared pale, bruised and boneless. The clan of Yahoo-Devil-Devils shambled, rolled or duckwalked until they were all within reach of Mutton Chop. Bluey shuffled closer too. Pearl twisted in his paw as if she could somehow retreat from this unholy gathering. Mutton Chop lifted the man high in display, then took hold of his arm and turned it. The arm popped off from the shoulder socket.

Pearl screamed. Absently, as if to soothe, Bluey stroked and patted at her.

Mutton Chop presented the severed arm to Silver, who took it, tossed it into his mouth and worked it around and around. Finally, his lips pursed to extrude the bones, and he spat.

"Holy Mary," Big Stanley choked.

Pearl's body shook so violently that she had to grip Bluey's paw with all her strength to keep herself upright. Mutton Chop pulled off the man's other arm and gave it to One-Eye. A leg went to Mama, who broke it in half, giving the thigh to Titch who gnawed on it enthusiastically. The other thigh went to Farthing, the nursing mother. Bubs detached from the nipple and reached up. Farthing masticated the thigh, dribbled a dollop of bloodied meat onto a finger, and offered it to Bubs to suck.

The man's lower leg was passed to Bluey. The big toe had an ingrown toenail, and this banal little detail did more to unhinge Pearl's mind than the dismemberment itself. Holding the severed limb by the heel, Bluey slurped the meat off the bones like it was a chicken wing. Mutton Chop dropped what remained of the man – the head and torso – into its own mouth. Pearl pressed both hands against her ears to block out the chewing sounds and kicked frantically, desperately, madly.

"I want to go home," she cried, over and over. "I want to go home."

Silver made a barking noise, which commanded the attention of all the Yahoo-Devil-Devils. Silver lifted Reginald Smith in one hand, and with the other, began to strip the clothes from his body. The Yahoo-Devil-Devils held out their palms, waiting for their offerings.

Pearl's eyes rolled up. Overcome, she fell away into a pit of nothingness.

***

Mrs Smith had been correct: the passage of rampaging Yahoo-Devil-Devils descending the mountain had cut an unmistakable swathe through the bush. All Eddie had to do was follow this impromptu road and he would find Pearl at the end of it. She was alive. Eddie knew this in his heart. If Bluey hadn't killed her back at the sheep station, then he had no intention of killing her at all. It was those apples, Eddie decided, the decent kindness and trust Pearl had shown the monster. Yet an unwelcome thought kept intruding on Eddie's optimism – *what about the other Yahoo-Devil-Devils?* – but he chose again not to borrow trouble.

Christ, his neck felt cricked from twisting around in the seat for hours to look out the back window, but reverse gear was the fastest way to make it up this mountain. A headache cinched his scalp. As the approach of dawn seeped a little colour into the moonlit landscape and birds started calling to each other, Eddie worried about the amount of petrol left in the tank. Reversing on an incline must be gulping fuel. Soon, the engine would cough and splutter, forcing them to stop and bust out a fuel can – and they only had two. How far away was Pearl? Would they have enough petrol to reach her? And if so, enough to speed back down the mountain, no doubt with Yahoo-Devil-Devils in hot pursuit? The sweat broke out across Eddie's back. Hell's bells, he had to stop tormenting himself with *what-ifs*. Just drive the motorcar, he told himself, and tackle one problem at a time.

"Hey, would ya look at that!" Jack said.

Eddie glanced out the front windscreen and his eyebrows shot up in surprise. "Hopper?"

"I figured he'd buggered off for good," Jack said, laughing. "Look, Dot. It's your mate!"

He reached into the back seat and plucked the terrier from her vigil to show her the kangaroo lolloping up the hill after them. Dot began to bark in excitement.

"Hopper's come to help us get Big Stanley," Mavis said, her voice thickening.

"We don't know what happened to him," Eddie said. "Maybe he got to the Smith house or stable."

Mavis glared. "To hide like a coward? No fucken way. Not my Big Stan."

She knuckled at her eyes. Taken aback, Eddie realised this tough old sheila was *crying*. But she could weather a beating in the tent without giving a goddamn, was a grouchy so-and-so at the best of times, and always seemed impatient with Big Stanley. Not knowing where he might be was a terrible concern, but still…why switch on the waterworks?

“Hey, what’s the matter?” he began, but she cut him off.

“Shut the fuck up,” she snapped. “And don’t look at me.”

“Jeez, I can’t help it. You’re in the back seat and I have to look out the back window—”

“Then keep your eyes fixed on the fucken window. Quit gawping.”

What the hell was happening right now? Confused and uncertain, Eddie glanced at Jack.

Jack shrugged and pulled his mouth into a sad smile. “They’re sweethearts.”

Sweethearts?

Mavis and Big Stanley?

It hardly seemed possible. Eddie had been with the troupe for a month and hadn’t seen any lovey-dovey behaviour pass between them. Yes, they smeared petroleum jelly on each other’s eyebrows and cheeks before every fight, but that seemed a professional courtesy. As did the strapping of each other’s broken fingers, the stitching of cuts. At dinner, they often divvied up: Mavis especially liked carrot, so Big Stanley would put some of his share onto her plate, while Mavis gave him her chops to gnaw. And sure, they always sat together at night, alone by the edge of camp, drinking their coffee…

Eddie’s cheeks flamed. Proof of love wasn’t in grand gestures like buying a half-dozen dresses from an emporium. It was in little things. Quiet things. In things that mattered.

“We’ll find Big Stanley,” Eddie said. “Don’t you worry, Mavis. We’ll find him.”

The sob that broke from her almost broke Eddie’s heart.

***

The harrowing screams of Big Stanley shocked Pearl awake. Good God. For a moment, she couldn't believe this horror was the real world and not a nightmare or the depths of Hell itself. One-Eye had torn off Big Stanley's right arm. The ritual of sharing the spoils was beginning again. Pearl writhed in Bluey's grip and shrieked piteously at the sky.

She wouldn't look as Big Stanley was ripped apart.

No, she couldn't look.

Dropping into a half-faint, she looked inward instead, recalling when she had turned up at the boxing tent with her cardboard suitcase. It had been a few hours before the evening session. Big Stanley noticed her and made his way over. She cowered before this burly, thuggish man with his broken nose and cauliflower ears, but his demeanour was courteous.

"Looking for work, love?" he said.

She nodded, feeling hopeless, pathetic. Trying to smile, she said, "I can wash and iron. I'm good at sewing too. I could mend that tent as good as new if you've got a big enough awl."

"The problem is that I sew quite well myself." He winked. "How's your cooking?"

"Oh, tip top. Damper, stews, eggs any which way, fruit pies. I make a tasty soup out of nothing but rainwater, scraps and turnip heads if ever the money's scarce."

He gently took her suitcase in his meaty hand. "Sounds good. What's your name, child?"

"Miss Pearl Bennett."

"That's a pretty name. All right, Pearl, let's get you introduced to the boss of this outfit, a certain Mrs Florence Taylor. She's got airs and graces. I'd advise you to put on an 'upstairs-downstairs' show, if you know what I mean." He began to walk and she hurried to follow. "Mrs Taylor's favourite dinner is Irish stew, so be sure to mention that. We're still-towning next at a sheep station, which means you can show off your skills with that particular recipe."

Oh, thank God for Big Stanley. He'd got her the job, convincing Florence despite the old woman's reservations against hiring a 'young and silly flibbertigibbet'. Such a kind man...

Pearl fought against the unwelcome return to reality.

The noises. She couldn't block out the *noises*.

The sound of munching and crunching made her gag, and still, Pearl didn't open her eyes. Her turn was next. So be it. Death would be a welcome relief.

Violent motion whiplashed her head. Gripping at Bluey's paw in an attempt to stabilise herself, she saw that he was backing up at a trot, waving his other arm with fingers clawed, making *uh-uh-uh* sounds and growling. The snarls of the other Yahoo-Devil-Devils started up and soon reached a terrific fever pitch. Pearl clamped her ears. Bluey snarled back.

She looked up at his jutting chin. Why, he was shaking his head at them!

The Yahoo-Devil-Devils crowded together, frowning, vicious, baring teeth, holding out their hands and gesturing impatiently. Realisation shot through Pearl in a flash. It was her turn to be dismembered and eaten, yet Bluey was refusing. Dear God! The other animals were so huge, so furious. How could he deny them when he was a lone youngster?

Silver stood to his full height of some twelve feet, raised his arms, and pounded at the ground with both fists. Bluey remained unmoved. In response, Silver charged about in a tight circle. He leapt high, ripped a branch from a mountain ash, and flung it like a javelin into the bush, all while panting and roaring. Still, Bluey held fast. Silver stopped to regard him.

Heads bowed, the other Yahoo-Devil-Devils moved back silently, as if to allow space.

Silver planted his feet and thudded his knuckles into the earth. He stared at Bluey without blinking. When he narrowed his eyes, Pearl could hardly breathe. What now?

Oh God, *what now?*

Bluey turned and ran.

He ran one-fisted, the knuckles of his free hand acting to pivot his lumbering feet across the ground at speed. Pearl bounced and jounced in his other paw. In any moment, her neck would break. She felt a falling sensation as if travelling down a slope. Cold water broke about her body. Gasping, she opened her eyes.

A river.

Bluey had fled into a river.

On the bank, the other Yahoo-Devil-Devils regarded him with hostility, outrage. There was much shouting back and forth. The volume of Bluey's violent roars concussed Pearl's eardrums. At last, as if disgusted, insulted but resigned, Silver lifted one dismissive arm and waggled his hand, barking and glaring about, until the other beasts acquiesced and lost their fury. Slack-shouldered, they turned and ambled into the bush.

Perhaps this meant Pearl was safe from being eaten. At least, for now. Bluey must have convinced his clan that he wanted her as a pet. Maybe he was planning to let her go instead? Return her to the Smiths' station? Or perhaps he wanted to consume her alone and in private. Oh God, who could fathom the mind of a savage man-beast?

Ha-ha-ha, Bluey seemed to laugh, and lifted Pearl level with his face.

Stunned, she drooped in his paw and waited for whatever torture would come next.

And the next torture came quickly.

Bluey frolicked and twirled about in the water. Pearl remembered that he'd been captured nearly one year ago, which meant it had been nearly one year since Bluey had bathed. The slow-flowing river was the colour of bitter stewed tea because of eucalypt tannins. If there were dangers like giant cod, barramundi, pincered yabbies or submerged branches, she had no hope of seeing them. The fear of dark water made her skin crawl, her breath short. As Bluey swirled about, Pearl's legs dragged helplessly in the chill water, this way and that.

Then he let her go.

Water closed over her head. Pearl didn't know how to swim. How would she? Swimming was an unconventional, rare skill. The irony wasn't lost on her: kidnapped by an omnivorous Yahoo-Devil-Devil yet dying by drowning. She struggled in vain, feeling herself sink. Thrashing, she opened her eyes. Down here, the water wasn't dark brown at all. It was a light tan, mostly clear with specks floating in suspension. Opalescent shapes, large and small, approached and shot past her; inquisitive fish that didn't care a jot if she lived or died, that would soon peck happily at the meat of her dead, bloated face.

The river bottom was sludge.

Her final resting place would be anonymous, muddy sludge.

She sank further, lungs convulsing. She looked up. At the surface, sunlight played on the rippling waves. Pearl thought about Mum, and shied away from those recent memories. Instead, she thought about Grandma, who had done her best during Pearl's childhood despite her lack of affection for Pearl, her resentment at another mouth to feed. Then Pearl thought about Big Stanley. Then Eddie and the ribbon he had bought her. How Eddie had patiently explained the motorcar and driven her through town purely for her enjoyment despite Florence awaiting his return. Eddie's large blue eyes, shy deference, his strong and beautiful hands. Oh yes, Pearl had known kindness in her short life. Drowning wasn't so bad...

Bluey's fingers closed about her. A rush of water pressed down on her head and shoulders.

Suddenly, she was breathing air. Coughing, choking, sucking oxygen. Pearl swiped at her eyes and snorted water from her nose. Bluey's lips mimicked a smile. He hooted a light *ha-ha-ha* as if this torture was all fun and games, which infuriated her beyond measure.

"You almost killed me in this bloody river!" she cried. "Damn you!"

Bluey lifted her clear and kissed the top of her head.

Breaking into sobs, relieved to be alive, Pearl grabbed at his face. His skin felt surprisingly human. "Thank you for not letting me die," she murmured, shivering full-length.

He strode out of the river. Exhausted beyond measure, Pearl wilted in his hand.

When she rallied, they were back in the clearing. There was no trace of Big Stanley. Dear God, she thought despairingly, the beasts have devoured him to the last morsel. She wept. Bluey murmured at her and touched her face, obviously puzzled by her distress. Oh, how could such an animal ever understand the horror, the grief? She kept pushing away his finger. Giving up at last, he grunted and popped out his bottom lip as if sulking. What a child! A bloody stupid child! She wanted to upbraid him, but how could she make him understand her anguish? Big Stanley was *dead.* So was Mr Smith and his worker.

Which left…Pearl.

A cold realisation of dread stiffened her limbs. Only then did she become aware of the other Yahoo-Devil-Devils. They seemed aggrieved. They had their backs turned on Bluey with their arms crossed. Occasionally, they looked around at him and scowled. Oh God, they still wanted to eat her. They were pressuring Bluey to comply. How long could he hold out against them? He was a youngster. How long before he gave in?

“Let me go,” she demanded, over and over, pushing against his thumb.

Until, snarling, he frowned down at her. In a flush of terror, she understood that if she angered Bluey enough, he might just serve her up to his clan, piece by piece. Remorseful, in a fit of desperate weeping, she grabbed his wrist.

“Please,” she sobbed, stroking at his ginger hair still damp from the river. “Don’t kill me.”

Trying to arrange her face into an appealing expression, she stared up at him and spoke tender nonsense.

Finally, his eyebrows relaxed and his mouth curved into a grin. He tickled beneath her jaw. She made herself laugh *ha-ha-ha*. This seemed to please him.

Stroking his paw with tender solicitude, her eyes twinkling wet with tears and fury, she sweetly sang, “Oh, you damned brute. You goddamned, flea-bitten, stupid brute!”

5.

The Model T stuttered, lost some ground, and backfired. Eddie gritted his teeth. The car coughed and stopped. Eddie adjusted the engine levers, engaged the brake, and jumped out.

"I've got to fill up the tank," he said, and then saw the danger.

A pack of dingoes.

Six of them.

Eddie froze. They looked like dogs, sleek and hard-bodied, with short fur coloured a light tan. Dingoes didn't bark, which was eerie, as if they weren't dogs at all but ghosts. Spirits ready to charge. Hopper bounced about, kept leaning back on his tail to punch his paws and kick, eager to fight. Kangaroos and dingoes were natural enemies. Undeterred, the dingoes dipped their heads and advanced, slowly, together making a whining purr. Eddie drew the gun from his waistband. In a pack, these wild native dogs could kill within seconds.

A car door opened. Eddie glanced back as Jack alighted with a rifle. Mavis, still in the car, had a Martini-Henry balanced on the window sill, one eye screwed shut as she sighted along the barrel.

Eddie said, "Don't waste the cartridges. We'll need every one of 'em for the Yahoo-Devil-Devils. Let me deal with these mongrels."

He'd never before fired a six-shooter but he knew to cock the hammer first, which he did with his thumb. Six dingoes, six bullets. Could he aim straight enough?

As it happened, there was no need to find out.

The sudden clopping of hooves startled the pack. The dingoes turned and tore off into the bush. So, the pack had lost their fear of humans but not horses. Which meant that somewhere in the pack's foraging area lived a family of dumb folks, too poor to own horses or mules, who were leaving out food for these dingoes, unaware that doing so made the animals much more dangerous. Eddie uncocked the hammer, put the gun in his waistband and peered about. There. About thirty feet away, a horseman was descending through the scrub.

"Hey, mate!" Eddie called, waving both arms. "Hey!"

The rider, a small man with whiskers, pulled the reins and cantered over to the car. Mavis got out and stood next to Eddie and Jack. The horse walked with clipped and high steps as if jittery, ready to bolt. Perhaps it was unnerved by Hopper's steady gaze. Or Dot's yapping.

"Can we shut up that bloody dog?" Eddie said, frowning at Mavis.

"Dunno," she snapped, hands on hips. "Feel free to give it a try."

Eddie sighed. For the love of Christ, Mavis was a touchy old woman. As soon as the rider came close enough, Eddie said, "You're one of Smith's men, right? One of the rescue party?"

The man nodded. His face was sweaty and wan, stricken.

Eddie's gut tightened. "What happened up there?"

The man lifted his hat, wiped his forehead with his forearm, and clamped his hat back on his head.

Meanwhile, the horse pawed the ground with white and rolling eyes.

"Mister?" Eddie said, alarm rising. "What happened?"

"It stinks," he said at last.

"What does?" Mavis said.

"The trail. Stinks of man-beasts. Some horses can take it, others can't. My horse can't. Poor Belle here has a delicate constitution. She's scared half to death."

The rider spat and wiped his mouth, his own frightened eyes also rolling in his head. Eddie suspected that perhaps the decision to ditch the rescue mission wasn't wholly that of Belle's.

"How far did you get?" Jack said.

"What?"

"How close to the Yahoo-Devil-Devils did you get before you decided to turn around?"

The rider's eyes focused. He appeared to see them all for the first time. His face set and scowled. He put a hand on the rifle. "Sounds like you're calling me a coward."

Eddie tensed. Oh hell, a proud and trigger-happy idiot was the last thing they needed—

"Listen, scout," Mavis said, stepping forward. "We're fucken glad to have met you. Tell us their position, number and movement before you head into town for reinforcements."

The change that came over the rider's face showed that Mavis had defused the situation. Damn. Eddie had never thought of Mavis as particularly clever, but right now, if she wasn't just the quickest-thinking woman he'd ever known in his life! The rider pointed up the hill.

"See that ridge? Go north-west about a mile or so until the ground dips into a basin. I figure it heads towards a river. Well, that's where the devils are, I reckon. In the basin. The other three riders are there. Should be there by now, though I haven't heard any shots."

"Are the captives alive?" Jack said.

The rider took affront. "How the fuck should I know? Didn't you hear me? I couldn't go any further on account of my horse."

Jack hawked and spat. "Yeah. I heard you."

The rider's cheeks coloured.

"What about remains?" Eddie added quickly. "Blood? Bones?" He faltered. "Heads?"

"Not a sign. Looks to me like the man-beasts carried their captives alive. Whether or not they're still alive this minute is anyone's guess, but I know which way I'd bet. Dead. Each and every one. Those monsters might keep to themselves, but whenever they encounter people, they like to eat 'em. Did you see what they did back at the station?"

"Yeah, we saw," Eddie muttered.

"Biting off heads," the rider continued, his eyes starting to glaze over, "busting up bodies. Chewing 'em for fun. Shit. Our best shearer, Jared Pilkington, got mashed through a man-beast's fist like a…like a goddamned *banana*—"

"Thanks, mate," Mavis said. "We appreciate your telling us which way to go. Now hurry into town and tell the cavalry, okay?"

"Huh?" the man said, as if coming to his senses.

"Mrs Smith is in town right now cobbling together a posse," Mavis said. "Tell them what you know. And can you tell them a rescue team from Taylor's Travelling Troupe is almost at the basin?"

"Sure I can."

"You'd better shake a leg. Godspeed."

Lifting his hat, the rider spurred his horse, which broke into a run down the mountain. They watched him depart. Within moments, the clopping of hooves faded away, deadened by the layers of trees, bushes and shrubs all around this outback countryside.

"You're amazing," Eddie said to Mavis. "That bloke would have shot us if not for you."

"Yeah, righto, keep your shirt on," she said gruffly, smiling despite her obvious attempts to hold a poker face. "Hurry, put the fucken petrol in the car."

Eddie hauled out the can. As he filled up the tank, he worried about Pearl. Felt sick about her. Of Big Stanley, he was sure the boxer had taken refuge somewhere about the homestead; Mrs Smith had overlooked him in her haste, that's all. The petrol glugged. Eddie perspired. If the remaining three men on horseback had reached the basin, why couldn't he hear gunshots? Had they *all* turned chicken? The thought of Pearl helpless amongst those beasts made Eddie want to tear out his hair.

The last of the petrol glugged into the tank. Eddie took out the can.

"Beauty," Jack said. "Nearly ready to go?"

"Yeah. I just have to chuck the empty can in the boot."

Clamping a firm hand on Eddie's shoulder, Jack said, "We'll get her back alive."

Jack's dark brown eyes were clear and steady, determined. Fearless. Eddie gripped the boxer's arm and nodded.

***

She was a bug in a jar. Thirsty with a dry and thickening tongue, hungry, distraught, Pearl lolled in Bluey's fist while he played with her hair. Frightened, assuming he would rip hanks of it from her scalp, she had initially shied away, struggling. But no, Bluey was gentle. She had given up all resistance. Now he trailed fingers through her locks, humming contentedly.

Meanwhile, the other Yahoo-Devil-Devils kept their backs turned. She and Bluey were *pariahs.* The situation made Pearl smile bitterly in recognition. Mum had been discreet with her drinking at first, but as years passed and Mum became an obvious drunkard, she and Pearl had received the cold shoulder from neighbours and soon from everyone, even the lowly dunny man whose job was to collect shit from the outhouses. Gossip travels fast in a small country town. And small-minded people are always the most judgemental.

So, these beasts understood concepts like shame and blame. Interesting. If Pearl survived – which she doubted – she could entertain people with her once-in-a-lifetime experience amongst Yahoo-Devil-Devils. The Taylor's Travelling Troupe would have a new attraction, presuming that Florence and Gilbert would rehire her. After all, she'd been sacked for removing Bluey's cage cover… She burned again with bitter remorse. Why oh *why* had she done such a stupid thing without considering what the consequences might be?

She saw Farthing, the drowsy Bubs at her breast, sit bolt upright.

Then Mama.

As the concerned females looked about the clearing, the adult males responded by standing in readiness. Silver, One-Eye and Mutton Chop cocked their heads. Bluey stopped fondling Pearl's hair. Not one beast moved a muscle. The tension telegraphed itself to Pearl and her heart thudded. Something was coming.

Something that posed a threat.

Another clan of Yahoo-Devil-Devils? Pearl had heard that clans often warred with one another, especially over territory disputes. Or issues much more scandalous. Rumour had it that a clan would raid another to capture adult females, which would bring about retaliatory battles from those invaded. Of course, Pearl wasn't supposed to know about this. Generally, men didn't discuss such indelicate matters in front of women, but Pearl had overheard the rumours on occasion when at bars purchasing gin for her mother.

If another clan of Yahoo-Devil-Devils burst into the clearing, Pearl was as good as dead. The fighting would be intense. She would be dropped or slapped from Bluey's grasp, crushed into the dirt by the scuffle of heavy feet, the fall of heavy bodies... Oh, so what? Weakly, she put her face in her hands. How many times would she have to brace for impending death? Maybe she just didn't care anymore.

The seconds ticked on.

Nothing.

Their continued motionless vigilance began to pull at her nerves.

Oh God, what were the beasts reacting to? With bated breath, Pearl strained her ears.

Nothing but the wind rustling through leaves—

Then she heard it.

Faintly.

Yes, far in the distance: the unmistakable tramp of horses' hooves.

Pearl's heart lifted. *Men.* Undoubtedly, men with guns. Men prepared to save her. At least, men who would risk their lives in the attempt. She prayed. For the rescuers, for herself. And, to her surprise, for Bluey too. Hadn't he been her protector throughout this nightmare? Shielding her from the teeth and gullets of his clan? Oh, but if only he'd saved Big Stanley. Yet Bluey had eaten Big Stanley with gusto… No, no, she could never forgive Bluey for that.

The adult males snuffled, snorted, dashed together on their knuckles towards the edge of the clearing, and paused there. Cautious. Sniffing. The females yammered in their strange gibber. Mama repeatedly swung her arm in a wild arc, perhaps urging the males to *go, investigate, charge*, while Titch climbed into her lap and huddled against her, chittering timidly, shivering, his eyes wide.

The way they acted was almost human. Their body language clear. Recognisable. *Relatable*. Pearl recalled Bluey's year of confinement in the Taylor's cage, Gilbert's three-pronged training harpoon, the collar and chain, Bluey's dutiful performance with Tom in the boxing tent, and her heart constricted in a sudden rush of pity. What appalling treatment he'd endured. Tears filled her eyes. No, she didn't want him shot. She wanted him free to live out his life in the wild; he deserved that much at least, after every pain and humiliation the Taylors had meted out. She patted at his thumb in sympathy for what he had gone through, and in fear of what he now might have to face. Bluey was too focused on assessing the threat to notice.

With an impatient gesture from Mama, Bluey got to his feet and joined the other males. Now Pearl had a better vantage point. Through the trees on the far ridge, backlit by the rising sun, were three riders on horseback. Could one of them be Eddie? He knew how to control a motorcar, and surely, that was a much more difficult skill than controlling a horse. Her spirits rose at the thought of seeing him again. Once reunited, she would kiss him. Wrap her arms about his neck and kiss him immodestly, like she had wanted to do after their drive yesterday around town but which she had deemed too forward, too outrageous, too *soon*. If she survived this experience, she vowed to live every day as if it might be her last.

Riders on horseback thundered into the valley.

Yahoo-Devil-Devils roared.

Fear leapt into Pearl's throat. Oh, don't let one of the riders be Eddie! He might die, and she couldn't bear it. Couldn't bear the notion of him dying like Big Stanley. So, she decided firmly that Eddie *wasn't* amongst them. Instead, she convinced herself that these riders were strangers. Where they had come from, she had no idea – the sheep station or town? – yet each rider was armed. Reins in one hand, rifle in the other, they galloped their horses and closed the distance, hooves raising dust. Pearl's anxiety surged. What if Eddie *was* one of the riders? The Yahoo-Devil-Devils roared again, louder this time, as if in warning: *last chance to turn back, or die.*

Tears poured down Pearl's cheeks. Frantic for rescue, panic gripped her fast.

"Help me!" she screamed. "Over here! Help me!"

Silver beat at his chest. One-Eye and Mutton Chop followed suit. Mama and Farthing gathered their children and hurried from the clearing towards, Pearl assumed, their bolthole. Perhaps a cave or somewhere else deemed safe to hide...

What would Bluey do with Pearl? He wasn't an adult male, nor was he a child. What was his role in this clan? Would he retreat with her or carry her into battle?

Unexpectedly, he kissed the top of her head. On tiptoes, he lifted her high and put her some fifteen feet from the ground onto the bough of an old man gum. She had never before sat high in a tree – had never even climbed one – and before she'd had a chance to secure herself, he let go and loped off. Her buttocks slid from the bough. She was falling!

Pearl grabbed for branches, but failed to get purchase. Tough, spiky twigs whipped through her palms as she dropped. Suddenly, legs flailing and swinging through empty air, she found herself clinging to a reedy offshoot that swayed and creaked, sounding ready to snap at any moment. Yet it held. She panted, tried to contain her fright, to *think*. Could she haul herself up? No, no, she didn't have the upper-body strength. God, would she fall? She screamed.

Her scream called Bluey.

This time, he gathered her into both hands and arranged her again on the same highest bough that he could reach, his lower lip puckered, heavy brow creased in concentration and concern. Once she was seated, he nodded *ha-ha-ha*, and tore off into the scrub.

Sobbing, trembling, Pearl wrapped her arms about the trunk. From such a height, she had a clear view of the clash about to happen between riders and beasts. The two sides charged at each other. There would be bloodshed, carnage, terrible images of mutilation and death that would be etched forever into her memory, the stuff of nightmares. More than anything, Pearl wanted to close her eyes. Transfixed, however, she couldn't look away.

The Yahoo-Devil-Devils were big enough to snatch up the horses, but the horses were fast and nimble. Their accomplished riders could turn them on a sixpence. The men must be stockmen and drovers, accustomed to pivoting horses with precision, well used to mustering the random and scattering nature of livestock. Driving hundreds of animals across long distances was an undertaking that required great skill and teamwork. The horses seemed undaunted too. How? Of course, Australian stock horses were a hardy bunch – smart, agile, courageous, bred and raised to marshal farm animals – but hell's teeth! These Yahoo-Devil-Devils weren't anything like a flock of scatterbrained, docile sheep. How could the horses keep their nerve? Especially when they were so comparatively small?

Giant arms swung. Roars and growls rent the air. Gunshots echoed. It sounded just like the ghastly raid back at the sheep station, where poor Tom had been butchered right in front of her. If only Pearl could shut her ears against the terrifying noises. And there was Bluey, confused, floundering, trying to keep up with his male relatives but clearly out of his depth. A rider discharged his rifle. Bluey flinched as if hit and lost his balance.

"Bluey!" Pearl shrieked, aghast.

To her relief, he quickly recovered. Oh, how on earth could she hate and fear him, yet feel so protective of him at the same time? It didn't make sense. There was no time to ponder. The riders appeared to have a strategy, working their horses in such a way as to encircle the beasts and bunch the Yahoo-Devil-Devils together, gathering them closer and closer. To shoot them like fish in a barrel, Pearl realised. What number of bullets would it take to bring down just one of those enormous Yahoo-Devil-Devils? Why, it would have to be dozens. Scores.

The shooting began in earnest.

Muzzle flashes from the rifles flared orange. A man would reload after every shot and focus his attention solely on the weapon, keeping in the saddle by the pressure of his knees, trusting his horse to dodge and weave on his behalf. Pearl had never before seen an equestrian team perform at the cutting edge of its ability. Over and over, a horse zoomed while its rider reloaded, the horse running full speed as if the uneven, stony ground held no dangers, the man lifting his rifle to shoot, the horse unperturbed and bold. Such an incredible sight! The display gave Pearl strength. The road to salvation lay in fearless, decisive action.

She would climb down this blasted tree. Peering, she tried to discern the best course.

The bellows of a Yahoo-Devil-Devil drew her attention.

It was Mutton Chop, recoiling and baulking. He sounded distressed rather than ferocious. Now she understood the full import of the riders' mustering strategy: they had decided to kill the Yahoo-Devil-Devils one at a time, and had chosen Mutton Chop to go first. Their strategy would succeed. Firstly, the three riders were still unharmed. Secondly, the dexterity of the horses confounded the Yahoo-Devil-Devils – one would reach out a giant hand only for the horse to switch direction and double back, too fast and nimble.

Oh, this was *nothing* like the slaughter back at the sheep station.

Stirred, Pearl gave an excited cheer. Victory was coming. She would soon be saved!

More gunshots. Mutton Chop staggered, dropping to a knee. Pearl cheered again. She thought of the poor man folded in half whom Mutton Chop had kept clasped within his simian feet before cruelly dismembering him. Her anger felt bracing.

"You demon!" she cried. "Go to hell!"

Mutton Chop regained his footing. Slow and slack-shouldered, he appeared bewildered. Bullets hit him repeatedly, pushing him this way and that – a dreadful sight to behold – yet he didn't retaliate. Pearl sagged, relief soothing her nerves like a balm. Oh, to be rescued…

Silver swung a paw. This manoeuvre turned out to be a feint. The beast's intended target was within reach of his *other* hand. Silver knocked down the horse and rider. Pearl gasped. Silver had worked out their strategy. Outfoxed them! Unmanned, the horse leapt to its hooves and shot at speed back up the hill. The rider scrambled and began to run, limping and hopping as if an ankle were broken. Where was his rifle? How could he defend himself? What would the other men do? Pearl's heart lodged in her throat.

The remaining two men on horseback tried distracting Silver to no avail. With single-minded purpose, Silver grabbed the downed rider. The man shrieked. As he was lifted to the beast's maw, Pearl glanced away, wrist at her mouth. The shrieking abruptly stopped. Pearl knew exactly what that meant. Pulse thudding in her ears, she risked another peek.

The tide of this battle had turned.

The two riders had lost their rhythm, their mustering circle apparently no longer possible.

Now, the Yahoo-Devil-Devils were chasing *them*.

Devastation sapped Pearl's resolve. Perhaps she ought to throw herself off this bough. Kill herself on her own terms. The only problem was that fifteen feet wasn't high enough to ensure death. She might only succeed in breaking her ankle like that poor, doomed rider...

Or could she still climb down? Try to make a run for it?

Pearl steeled herself.

Yes, she would climb down and run. What other choice did she have?

The bark felt cool and sharp. Her feet were bare. Somewhere between the sheep station and the home of the Yahoo-Devil-Devils, she had lost her sandals or been stripped of them. The rocky ground would cut her feet to pieces. No point worrying about that yet. First, she had to work her way along this blasted trunk.

The distant gunshots, growls and snarls went on and on. Descending the tree was slow, arduous work. Her toes had to grope for one branch after another. Sweat popped on her forehead. Could she shimmy instead? Cling to the trunk like a pole and slide? No, the trunk wasn't smooth enough, branches sprouted everywhere, and she was scared of falling. A flap of bark dislodged. A hand-sized huntsman spider reared its front legs, mandibles gnashing. Pearl cried out, and lost her grip. Tumbled, hit a bough with her hip, reached blindly and held on.

Winded, she tried to calm herself and gather her wits.

Could she push off and drop? No, the leaf litter still looked too far away. Dizziness washed over her and the ground reeled. The shooting had stopped. The battle must be over. Soon, the Yahoo-Devil-Devils would return, and Bluey would gather Pearl into his paw. She had to hurry.

Pearl forced her limbs to move. Quickly, quickly, she had to descend *faster*. Panting, sobbing, she judged the ground as close enough – more or less – and let go. The impact jarred her knees. She tumbled across the detritus. Scrabbling, she got up, too fired with adrenaline to check for injuries, and started running.

The sheep station lay east of here, but she had no time to take her bearings from the sun. Her limbs pumped like pistons. The rocks, fallen branches and thick grasses hurt her feet, cutting and bruising them, yet she couldn't afford to pick her way through the undergrowth.

Speed, speed, speed. Objects loomed in her vision and zigzagged past: tilting trees, startled wallabies, birds taking flight. In the red dirt ahead flashed the glossy, slithering coils of a snake – a deadly brown snake – and somehow her legs found the ability to leap her clear even before her mind had processed the danger.

Panting, her dry mouth felt like cotton, her tongue swollen. Dehydration pounded a sickening headache behind her eyes. Her joints felt weak and loose, rubbery. None of these things mattered. *Speed, speed, speed.* Pearl was running for her life and she knew it.

6.

A throaty snarl sounded behind her. Pearl's body flooded with enough adrenaline to supercharge her heart. Now, she flew between the trees. And if her feet were getting sliced to the bone, she had no idea, for she could no longer feel pain. Her vision pinned. On every step, all she saw was the furthest distance through the bush ahead. The entirety of her being was focused on reaching that furthest distance.

The snarling sounded closer and the earth trembled.

Galvanised, Pearl took even longer strides, even as ligament fibres stretched and snapped.

With a rush of air that fluttered Pearl's tresses about her face, a great shadow passed overhead and landed in front of her. The force of its landing rocked the ground and threw up a huge raft of leaf litter. Pearl skidded to a halt and fell back, sitting heavily. She could hardly believe her eyes at the vision. Was she hallucinating?

Silver.

He had leapfrogged her, blocking her escape. Splotches of blood covered his shaggy hide. His open mouth showed long teeth, furred tongue, gaping throat. Resting his weight on his knuckles, he leaned over and roared. His stinking breath blew her hair back from her face. Pearl collapsed, stunned. After a moment, Silver stood to his full height and sneered down at her, his chest rising and falling with effort.

Now she would die.

He would consume her, like he had planned from the beginning of her captivity. Bluey must be dead or badly injured. The two remaining riders must be dead too. All was lost.

Silver snorted a hard, contemptuous breath through his nostrils. Reached out his hand. Pearl didn't bother to close her eyes. No, she was beyond care or sanity now.

***

Eddie jolted in the driver's seat, the cigarette dropping from his lips. Gunshots! The Smiths' rescue party had at last encountered the Yahoo-Devil-Devils. Eddie pressed harder on the pedal. Rocking, the Model T powered up the slope. If only Dot would stop her infernal barking.

"Look out, mate," Jack said. "There's a boulder in your way."

He and Mavis had been backseat-driving this whole bloody time. Neither of them had any idea how to work a motorcar. Couldn't Eddie do his job without copping pinheaded feedback from the ignorant? Infuriated, he planted his foot. The engine revved. A back wheel hit the boulder. The car lifted, leaning on a precarious angle. Jack and Mavis cried out in alarm.

"Fuck!" Eddie said through teeth, and slammed levers, pressing the forward pedal.

The wheel rolled off the boulder and bounced onto the ground. Unsettled, the car bucked and teetered, careening down the hill as it fishtailed, threatening to tip. Eddie had to let the machine settle before braking or else he'd tip it for sure.

"Where the hell are you going?" Jack shouted.

"Yeah, stop and back up!" Mavis added.

The car regained its equilibrium. Braking, Eddie shouted, "Can you two do a better job? No? Then quit bitching and let me drive this goddamned thing!"

"But can't you hear the shooting?" Jack said.

"All I can hear is you arseholes nagging me about how to drive. Now shut up, or God help me, you can both get out and walk. And somebody shut up that dog!"

He stamped the reverse pedal and weaved the car along the hill's summit towards its ridge, hoping to gather enough momentum to make it up and over the lip. The car bumped and bounced. Stones, rabbit holes, exposed tree roots, fallen branches, so many hazards cloaked beneath fallen leaves. Eddie had to *feel* the ground through the wheels, respond instantly to the kick and spin of the steering. It required intense concentration. These past hours of driving this hill backwards had given him the mother of all headaches.

"Keep that dog quiet, for the love of Christ," he snapped.

Jack gathered Dot into his arms and patted at her absently, stroking her ears, trying to soothe her.

Perhaps Dot was so excitable because she could smell Pearl's scent… Pearl *must* be alive, Eddie decided. She just *had* to be.

A flash went past the windows, startling him. But it was only Hopper, going on ahead. The car engine whined. The hill's summit was too steep. Eddie desperately worked the levers. Perspiration swamped his armpits. The engine screamed yet the car was slowing down.

"Can't you go any faster?" Mavis said.

"Oh, sure," Eddie retorted. "Like a bat out of hell if I wanted to. I'm just being contrary."

She scowled at him. Then he noticed she was sweating too. So was Jack. Everyone's nerves were stretched tight. No one had slept, the anxieties of this rescue mission were considerable, and now the constant rifle fire and roars of Yahoo-Devil-Devils had them all close to bursting point—

One of the wheels lost purchase. The car teetered and spun a little. Eddie wrestled to steer. Here we go, he thought darkly, we're about to tip over and slide the whole way down the hill.

But the wheel gripped. The car found traction.

With a jouncing burst of speed, it went up and over the ridge, and landed neatly on level ground. Success! Eddie engaged the brake and cut the motor. Jack and Mavis were already leaping from the car, rifles in hand. Eddie took a half-minute to roll and light a smoke with trembling fingers, to brace himself for whatever horrific sight he was about to confront, including the sight of Pearl lying broken and mutilated. If she was alive and he managed to rescue her, he'd kiss her right on the mouth. He'd wanted to kiss her at the haberdashery yesterday, but lacked the nerve. What a fool! Hadn't he already known that today was all you could ever have and that tomorrow might never come?

Grabbing a Martini-Henry and a box of cartridges, he got out of the car.

Below was a narrow valley. The land in the foreground lay flat and sparsely forested. On one side of the valley ran a wide and slow-moving river. On the other side raged a battle that any rational person would never believe unless they saw it with their own eyes.

Horsemen riding pell-mell, shooting. A Yahoo-Devil-Devil on its stomach, rolling about with its arms folded beneath its body, obviously wounded and in pain. Two giant Yahoo-Devil-Devils lunging and batting at the horsemen, too slow to make contact. Eddie recognised those Yahoos from the station: the beast with silvering hair, and the abomination with one eye that had slaughtered Tom. Unless the horsemen finished the job right here and now, Eddie determined to avenge Tom and kill that one-eyed bastard himself.

And in the midst of the melee stood Bluey, small in comparison to his relatives, acting confounded and at a loss. He was a spectator rather than a participant, doing little more than spinning about to keep the horsemen in sight.

The riders were fleet and nimble. Yet there were only two of them. Weren't there supposed to be three? Where was the third? Had he turned back, like the coward they'd encountered on the hillside? More to the point, where was Pearl? Blood spattered the ground, but Eddie decided the blood was from the wounded Yahoo-Devil-Devil. Pearl was alive until proven otherwise. Then it occurred to him that he, Jack and Mavis were all standing motionless, stunned and paralysed, just goggling at the spectacle playing out below.

"Well, come on," he said, breaking the spell. "What's our plan?"

"Should we try to shoot?" Mavis said.

"Not from here," Jack said. "Too far. It'd be a waste of bullets."

"Then what's the plan?" Eddie said. "We can't drive into the valley. They'd see us. That silver one would mash the car like he did back at the station."

"Maybe we can take the long way round," Jack suggested, pointing, "through those trees for camouflage. I reckon the clan must live further back in that bush yonder."

"Where they've got Big Stanley and Pearl," Mavis said.

"So, we're decided," Eddie said. "If the monsters live and make a run for home, we'll follow but on a long tail. If all the monsters are killed, we'll head straight back there—*no!*"

The one-eyed bastard had clipped the legs of a passing horse and brought it down.

Eddie lifted the rifle, his urge to shoot in defence of the rider momentarily stronger than logic. Jack pushed aside Eddie's rifle barrel. The horse got up and bolted. Shit, the rider's foot was caught in the stirrup! At full gallop, the horse tore away from the battle, dragging the rider along, his body rattling and thumping over the ground, his head bouncing against stones like a loose ball on a string. Eddie felt sick.

"Holy Mother of God," Jack whispered. "That poor bloke."

Mavis said grimly, "Don't worry, he can't feel it. He's already dead."

The remaining rider snapped the reins, dug in his boots and took off in pursuit. He had no chance of catching up. In a flash, the dragged rider was swallowed by the bush. Thwarted, the horseman came to a halt. He turned his steed this way and that, as if unsure of what to do next. The Yahoo-Devil-Devils had lost interest in him, were now gathering about their fallen kin. Surely, the horseman couldn't ride back and take them on alone?

Inspiration struck Eddie. "We'll signal him!" he said, and taking Tom's gun from his waistband, aimed into the sky and pulled the trigger. The shot echoed around the valley. The remaining rider took up his reins, spurred his horse, and rode towards them, raising dust.

Jack turned on Eddie, face twisting. "Dickhead! You've signalled the Devils too!"

Oh shit. Eddie hadn't thought of that. Since they were standing on a ridge, the reddened sky of sunrise must be silhouetting their forms in sharp relief. But if the Yahoo-Devil-Devils had seen them, they didn't care. The one-eyed bastard was leaned over the beast writhing on the ground, prodding at him with a tentative hand. The silver beast retreated into the valley, heading for the clutch of forest towards its presumed home. Bluey followed, head down.

Meanwhile, the horse negotiated the steep slope with ease. The rider was amongst them and hauling on the reins while the horse, mouth foaming, huffed and pawed at the ground.

"Christ, are youse *it*?" the rider demanded, his wild face streaked in dirt and sweat.

"Are we what?" Mavis said.

"The posse," he continued, panting. "Mrs Smith told us she'd go to town and get one together. Hell, if you ain't the lamest fucken posse I've ever seen in my life. Is that damned kangaroo part of your crew, or what? Shoo, you piece of vermin. Shoo!"

"Leave him alone," Jack retorted. "Yeah, he's with us."

Mavis said, "Mrs Smith *did* go to town. Maybe she's sending a posse our way right now."

"Then who the fuck are you fellas?"

"Workers from Taylor's Travelling Troupe," Eddie said.

"Youse are the boxers? Okay. I see you got rifles. You got horses?"

"We came by motorcar," Eddie said. "Listen, the beasts took prisoners. Did you see any?"

"No, but I reckon I heard a woman scream for help."

Eddie felt dizzy with hope and desperation. Pearl was alive!

"So, how are we going to tackle this?" Mavis said.

The rider spat. "If you ain't got horses, we're no match for those demons. We wait for the posse. With numbers on our side, we can go in for the kill. Take out the whole clan, females and children too. And quick, before the buggers think to take revenge on the town for *that*."

He jerked his thumb to indicate the felled Yahoo-Devil-Devil. The one-eyed bastard had turned it over onto its back, and was trying to haul the beast upright, with no luck.

High-pitched barking drew their attention. Eddie turned in time to see Dot jump from an open window of the Model T and start running.

"Hey, come back here!" Jack called. "Dot!"

Ignoring him, the little terrier ran past and scampered down the hillside into the valley.

***

Rigid with disbelief and dismay, Mrs Reginald Smith looked around at the men who crowded the governor's office. She knew them all. Respectable, well-heeled and sober men. In turn, they knew her and Reginald, had broken bread with them at various dinners, shared wine. There sat the governor, police sergeant, priest, doctor, barber, tailor, grocer, haberdasher—

"Edna," the governor was saying, addressing her by her first name, which in itself was a patronising insult, "Edna, you must see this situation from our point of view."

She had come to town in her nightgown and coat, dishevelled, trotting her pony along the main street and sideroads, pleading for help at the top of her lungs. Sugar, her steadfast little pony, was almost dead from exhaustion. With head bowed, Sugar was now hitched to a post outside. It had taken an unbelievably long time to drag the townsfolk out of their beds for this impromptu assembly, even with the priest ringing the church bell. Mrs Smith couldn't understand the mood in the room. The *reluctance.* She had badly injured men back at the station. Why wasn't the doctor hastening in his carriage to their aid? Why was he sitting here in the governor's office, avoiding her eye? None of this made sense.

"Thank you, Governor," she said. "If you wouldn't mind, please explain your point of view to me, since I'm failing to grasp it."

The men shifted around and glanced at each other. Next to her sat George, one of her classers who graded the shorn fleeces. He had been part of the four-man rescue team, but his horse's fear had driven him back despite his repeated spurring. The Yahoo-Devil-Devils have a stink which was apparently too much for George's filly to bear. Fair enough. At least George was sitting beside Mrs Smith to help her persuade the town to take action. Helping but failing. According to George, a rabble from the boxing troupe was halfway up the mountain range in a Model T, intent on rescue. Well, that was better than nothing. Better than these respectable men in their collared shirts, ties and jackets showing their yellow colours with every weaselling word that dropped from their lips.

George stood. "Didn't you hear the lady? She asked you to explain your point of view!"

The men coughed and muttered. Behind them sat the most well-respected women, among them the milliner, dressmaker, teacher, boarding-house owner—

"The safety of this town depends on one thing," the police sergeant said. "Mutual respect between species. Don't you remember your history? The massacre of 1903? The people who expanded this place from a settlement into a town figured they'd first drive out the mountain clan of Yahoo-Devil-Devils. They paid a heavy price for their hubris. If we stage an offensive, the clan would most likely retaliate and everyone in town and the surrounding districts would be in danger. The number one rule: we leave them alone; they leave us alone."

"*They leave us alone?*" Mrs Smith said. "Those monsters kidnapped my husband. One of my shearers too. They killed and injured many others. And you would do nothing?"

More muttering. Was it her unbrushed hair? The lace hem of her knee-length nightgown peeping out from beneath her coat? Her bare shins above the boots? Did they think she was drunk or crazy? All right. Mrs Smith's mind was made up. She would go outside, stand on the steps and address the crowd. The rest of the town was gathered in the square, every man and woman terrified, anxious to know what was going on, huddled together; agricultural workers and salespeople and servants who were no doubt a damn sight more blessed with backbone than these mealy-mouthed saps who would rather let Reginald die than lift a gosh-darned finger—

"It's not that we *want* to sit on our hands, Edna," the governor said, "it's just that, to be honest, there's nothing we *can* do. Even if we mounted an offensive, a successful outcome is unlikely. They're bush creatures. While they remain in the bush, they have the advantage."

"Consider the logistics," the police sergeant said. "How would we even reach them?"

"On horseback," she replied.

"Yes, but…" The police sergeant blushed and looked around for support.

"Edna, please," the doctor said, "be reasonable. Everyone here shares your pain. Offers their sympathy. But the hard, cruel fact remains that we all know what Yahoo-Devil-Devils like to do with captured people. And it's been many hours since the attack on your station." He ran his hands across his thinning hair, darted his eyes about the room, and continued, "Any rescue mission would be a folly. We can't risk more lives for no purpose."

No purpose.

Galled, Mrs Smith thought of the many times they had received the doctor and his wife in their dining room, the many sides of lamb gifted to them in friendship.

"If it were your spouse," Mrs Smith said, "I doubt you'd have the same opinion."

Murmurs rippled throughout the room.

The dressmaker stood up and said in a loud voice, "No one else will admit the truth, but I will. Mrs Smith, you invited the trouble yourself! The boxing troupe has a Yahoo-Devil-Devil in a cage, caught from regions around these parts."

"That could only cause trouble," someone else shouted.

"You can't deny it," said another.

"Clearly, the clan would come back to reclaim their own family member. You talk of your husband being kidnapped, but that Yahoo-Devil-Devil was kidnapped first!"

"Hear, hear," sounded various spirited voices.

"My husband didn't kidnap the blasted thing!" Mrs Smith cried.

"Hosting those that did on your property is as good as collusion," somebody said.

"Collusion? And who among you didn't buy a ticket, watch the fights and place a bet?" Mrs Smith said. "The tent was full both sessions, if I recall correctly. Most of you were there. I remember seeing you, and you, and you!" she added, pointing around the room. "According to such logic, there are no innocents in this town. By association, all of you are tainted and just as guilty as I am."

"Well, I certainly didn't attend that dreadful spectacle," the dressmaker said.

"Perhaps not," Mrs Smith said, "but you put the troupe's poster in your window."

"A piece of paper!" the dressmaker retorted. "I hardly see how taping a piece of paper to my window *as a favour* could be seen as anything other than an act of neighbourly kindness."

Voices swelled and chattered until the police sergeant stood up. Straightening his jacket, he declared, "Edna, the decision to host the troupe was yours and your husband's, not the town's. This was about personal gain. You wanted to make money and you certainly did."

A hostile mood descended. Smug and satisfied faces regarded her regally, self-righteously. Mrs Smith, swallowing her tears and rage, gazed at the vaulted ceiling of this opulent government office and wished for the old days. Back in her childhood, when bushrangers needed to be chased down and shot, men were brave and hot-blooded, ready to charge with guns. And now? Jelly-backs. Losers. She wanted to spit on them.

"Are you going to help me or not?" she said.

"Please understand, we'd like to help," the teacher said, "but the help you want in particular is futile. Your husband can't be saved. He's already dead. But there's plenty the town can do to lend a hand in future. For starters, we could find staff for your station—"

"I have staff at my station right now who are injured and dying," Mrs Smith said. "Why are they being denied medical help?"

Scoffing, eyes flashing, the doctor looked about for support. "I'm a member of the town's legislature. By sworn oath, I need to be part of any town meeting—"

"No! I've heard enough!" Mrs Smith stood up. Without another word, she swept from the room. Everyone began talking at once. Mrs Smith didn't care. She marched down the corridor, George hurrying at her heels. When she flung open the front doors and stood on the top of the steps, the gathered townsfolk hushed and looked up at her. So many frightened faces. They *ought* to be frightened, she thought. Demons from hell sat right on their stoops.

"My name is Mrs Reginald Smith," she proclaimed. "Most of you know me. My husband and I run the sheep station west of here."

People nodded, and an enthusiastic babbling ran across the crowd.

Encouraged, Mrs Smith continued, "Yahoo-Devil-Devils raided my station and kidnapped my husband and one of our men. They murdered and injured many others.

Four – no, three – of my men are in pursuit. Members of the visiting boxing troupe are also seeing what they can do out there. I need a posse of armed men to ride into the ranges and mount a full-scale rescue. Who's with me?"

The crowd's energy dropped. A few people at the back wandered off.

"You'd let the Yahoo-Devil-Devils win?" she cried. "No, we have to fight!"

The crowd began to disperse. Mrs Smith felt a sob rise in her throat. Someone touched her arm. It was George. Mrs Smith found the strength to lift her chin.

"Let's go, missus," he said.

"Already? We should try—"

"There's nothing we can do. We're licked, missus." George sighed. "Excuse my French but when it comes right down to it, most people are just selfish arseholes."

Taking her elbow, he aided her down the steps. At the hitching post were Sugar and George's horse, a filly named Belle. Drained, Mrs Smith rubbed at Sugar's nose and gazed into the pony's moist, brown and uncomprehending eyes. George looked up and down the street. Mrs Smith did too. The street was emptying of people. Doors were shutting. Everyone in town had decided to wash their hands of this horror, to pretend nothing had happened.

"So, there'll be no posse," Mrs Smith said.

George shook his head. "No posse."

Dawn. Across the square and beyond the rooftops of Main Street lay the distant mountain range, flat-topped, wreathed in its customary blueish haze that rose from the oil-bearing eucalypt forest. How strange that she had ended up living in the sticks. She was a city girl, born and reared in Sydney by English parents who had come by ship to forge a new life. They had often talked of the Old Country with its lush green countryside filled with squirrels, badgers and hedgehogs. They considered the Australian bush a death trap. Merciless hot sun, a central desert stocked with dangerous creatures including spiders, snakes, dingoes and especially Yahoo-Devil-Devils. When she'd accepted Reginald's marriage proposal and told her parents that she'd be mistress of an outback sheep station, they'd been aghast. *You'll regret it*, her mother wept. But Mrs Reginald Smith, captivated by the rigours and rewards of farming life, had never experienced a single regret.

Until now.

She closed her eyes and felt hot tears run down her cheeks. Poor Reginald. She thought of Vincent the kidnapped shearer, her three workers attempting a rescue, the boxing troupe doing their best with what little they had. Oh, was there any hope now?

"God help them all," she wept.

7.

Pearl, supine on the ground and panting from the exertions of her doomed flight, watched the approach of Silver's giant hand with detachment and mild curiosity. Why, she ought to be *screaming*. She knew then that she had lost her mind. Would he bite off her head, strip her limbs, or simply lob her through the air like a cricket ball? So many options. So many weird ways to die. In her young life, she hadn't given much thought to how she might expire, but death by Yahoo-Devil-Devil had never occurred to her.

Silver's palm was dark, heavily lined. Spattered with gore from the rider he'd killed. Hopefully, the rider's horse had got away. Silver's fingers splayed out. She could smell his hand: earthy, unwashed, sulphurous. Perhaps he would pick her up and squish her through his fingers. Pearl chuckled witlessly. Oh, what a strange end that would be—

A sudden harsh grunting, reminiscent of a pig, barked *uh-uh-uh!*

Like a child caught reaching into a biscuit tin, Silver retracted his hand in a flash and sat back. Pearl lifted herself onto her elbows and twisted around to see what he was looking at.

Mama.

Waddling along with Titch in her wake, Mama was frowning, lips pursed. *Uh-uh-uh!* she grunted again, repeatedly throwing out one long and hairy arm. *Go away*, she seemed to be telling Silver. *Back off*. Surprisingly, it worked. Silver actually shuffled aside a few feet. Then he gazed off into the bush as if bored. Trying to save face, Pearl surmised. Only then did she take notice of the injuries across his chest and belly. The riders had shot him many times, yet he didn't seem bothered. Perhaps the bullets hadn't penetrated far into his hide. Perhaps bullets were as bothersome to a Yahoo-Devil-Devil as mosquito bites to a human.

Mama was neither fooled nor placated by Silver's show of nonchalance. She went right up to him and began to yammer. He made soft, half-hearted noises in reply while refusing to meet her eye. Titch cuddled up to Mama's back, yowling. This was a family argument, Pearl realised, with none of the participants taking any notice of her.

Slowly, Pearl gained her feet.

Carefully, so as not to rustle the leaf litter.

And then she was off! Sprinting as fast as she could go, dodging trees, leaping over logs, the blood in her ears pounding like a hammer. A vision of the Smiths' kitchen swam into her mind, the pot of Irish stew bubbling on their wood stove, her remark to the missus: *A proper stove is such a blessing…* Pearl would soon be back there. Safe in that large spotless kitchen, sitting at the table with a blanket about her shoulders and a mug of hot sweetened tea in her hands. Or a cup and saucer instead of a mug? A fine, educated lady like Mrs Reginald Smith would most likely have cups and saucers—

Pearl was knocked to the ground. Winded, tumbling across dead leaves and twigs, she came to a stop and glanced up at her assailant, fearing Silver.

It was Mama.

Gibbering at Pearl, annoyed, exasperated, Mama was *upbraiding* her somehow. Behind Mama lurked Titch, picking his nose. No sign of Silver. As Mama continued to yammer, Pearl sat up. How would Mama kill? Would she behead or bite? Feed Pearl to Titch—?

"Oh, just get it over with!" Pearl shouted. "What the hell are you waiting for?"

Mama sat back on her heels as if shocked. Offended. Titch came out from behind Mama and approached, making soft tutting noises. Mama crossed her arms and looked away. Pearl shrank back. Titch fingered Pearl's hair, poked and prodded at her cautiously, lifted one of her legs and studied it with cross-eyed interest, his tongue extruded. Pearl sobbed in fright. Oh God, was he planning to bite off her toes? Suck the meat from her calf?

Before Titch could do anything more, Mama slapped his hand away.

A moment's grace!

Pearl flipped onto her stomach and scrambled, gathering her feet beneath her in order to run. A firm grip enclosed her lower legs. Over her shoulder, Pearl saw Mama's glowering face, the dark ape-like features arranged into an irritated and reproving glare.

"Let me go!" Pearl cried, struggling. "Please, let me go!"

No use. Mama began to waddle back through the bush. Good God! Bluey always held Pearl to his chest, cradling her with care, but Mama didn't give a damn. Holding Pearl by the legs, Mama trailed her through the dirt as if Pearl were a doll.

In desperation, Pearl tried to walk both hands across the ground to save herself from bumping over rocks and tree roots. No good. She reached up and gripped Mama's thumb, gasping, trying to hoist her body clear of the ground. Nearby toddled Titch, one finger again digging mindlessly inside his nose. His gaze was transfixed. If

Titch got hold of her, Pearl would die, regardless of his intentions. Once, she'd witnessed a child accidentally kill a kitten with rough and ignorant handling. Where was Bluey? Her only chance of survival was Bluey.

Tiring of walking on one set of knuckles, Mama soon decided to use both hands. With each step, Mama swung the arm that held Pearl. Despite her best efforts, worn out beyond endurance, Pearl was dragged through the dirt. Stones and sticks dug through her thin dress and tore into her skin. Her hair kept catching and pulling out from the scalp.

I'm going to die by degrees, Pearl despaired. One injury after another, after another—

Mama stopped.

Hurled Pearl by her legs through the air.

Pearl, too stunned to cry out, tumbled and wheeled, then landed with a thump against something warm and furry. She opened her eyes. Bluey! It was Bluey gazing down at her. Hooting softly, his lips curling into a smile, he gathered her into his hands. In relief, Pearl began to cry. She reached up and touched his face.

"Thank God," she whispered over and over.

Mouth pursed in concentration, he plucked the twigs and leaves from her person, taking extra care with her hair so as not to pull it. Using his thumb and forefinger, he gently lifted one of her bloodied hands for inspection. Then he inspected the other. Scowling, he hiccup-barked at Mama, who promptly screeched back and flapped an arm in Silver's direction. Pearl could almost hear Mama's affronted rebuttal: *How dare you blame me for your pet's injuries! If not for me, your pet would be dead! Silver wanted to kill it!*

Growling, Silver regarded Bluey with a sneering lip. Mama barked at Silver in reproach. Silver lifted his nose, stood up, and made a show of turning his back to sit down again.

Pearl made an educated guess at the family dynamics: Silver and Mama were a couple; their youngest was Titch, Bluey their eldest. Silver didn't approve of Bluey's 'infatuation' with Pearl who was, by Yahoo-Devil-Devil standards, the equivalent of a roasted chicken. Yet Bluey's mother vigorously supported her son's offbeat peccadillo. He had been missing for a year – no doubt she was so glad of his return that she would indulge any kind of behaviour, no matter how preposterous it may seem. Because Mama *loved* him.

Pearl began to laugh. Hysterically. Out of exhaustion and terror, yes, but out of disbelief too. All her life, she'd been taught that Yahoo-Devil-Devils were emotionless killing machines akin to crocodiles, yet Bluey's family was more functional than Pearl's own had *ever* been. Why, Pearl was an illegitimate who didn't even know her father's name!

"I'm sorry they kept you locked in a cage," she said, patting Bluey's thumb as fresh tears pricked her eyes. "It seemed awful before, but oh, it's so much more awful now."

He stroked her hair and crooned.

"If only you could understand me," she said forlornly.

For the first time, she noticed his gunshot wound – a raggedy clot in the chest near his shoulder, the hair matted with dried blood – and with a gasp, she pointed at it in alarm. He glanced at the wound. Tutting softly, he used his forefinger to nudge aside her extended arm as if to say, *don't worry, I'm all right.*

"How will you be all right," she argued, "if there's no doctor to dig out the bullet?"

Then Titch approached in a sidling fashion. Looked askance. Looked at Pearl. Looked askance again. Lifted his brows enquiringly at his older brother. What now? Pearl held her breath. With a grudging sigh, Bluey opened his hands – just a little – to allow Titch a glimpse of Pearl. However, as soon as Titch tried to poke a finger,

Bluey hugged her protectively against his chest and hissed. Titch recoiled.

Mama didn't seem to care about this slight towards her youngest. However, Farthing apparently did and barked a strange cough, over and over. Bluey poked out his tongue and blew a raspberry. Cuddled in Farthing's arms, Bubs made a sound much like a giggle, and blew enthusiastic raspberries in response. Bluey and Farthing began to laugh. These exchanges seemed self-explanatory, and yet…

Was Pearl *imagining* the humanness of these animal interactions? Dehydrated, starved, traumatised, frightened to death, could she trust her eyes and ears, her interpretations? Right now, was Pearl sane or insane? Such an existential question was too big to ponder. Weak and delirious, she hunkered against Bluey's chest and determined to go to sleep. In dreams, she would find refuge. God, she was weary. All she wanted to do was sleep. Sleep and dream…

A loud roar shocked her awake.

The Yahoo-Devil-Devils turned towards the same direction. One-Eye emerged from the bush, gesturing frantically. Sparked into action, Silver lurched onto his knuckles and was off at a trot, following One-Eye back towards the open valley. Pearl sat up in Bluey's hands. What on earth was going on? Then it dawned on her.

Where was Mutton Chop?

The same thought must have occurred to the others because they muttered and whined. Pearl had last seen Mutton Chop from her vantage point in the tree. The horseback riders had targeted him, shooting again and again, until he had dropped to one knee and then staggered upright, befuddled. Pearl had then descended the tree, with no idea of what had transpired.

A continuous noise of dry, rustling leaves got louder and closer.

Labouring, hauling a great weight behind them, Silver and One-Eye reached the clearing. Pearl knew their burden before she saw it. They dragged Mutton Chop to the centre of the clearing, each holding one of his wrists. Mutton Chop was on his back, limp and bloody, eyes closed, mouth agape, lips smeared in a slimy pink froth. Silver and One-Eye arranged his arms by his sides and stood back, regarding him with furrowed brows. Everyone stared at him quietly for a few moments. Was Mutton Chop dead or just unconscious?

The adults started to gabble and grumble at each other, making sharp, hard sounds. Silver pounded the earth and snarled. What was happening? They all seemed *furious*. Were they getting ready to fight? Scrambling, Pearl curled up inside Bluey's grasp.

Mama approached Mutton Chop. Farthing, little Bubs in arms, also shuffled closer. Bluey stayed put, and Pearl wondered if his failure to take part in this inspection might be interpreted as an insult. However, Silver and One-Eye had stepped back too. Perhaps this – whatever 'this' was – happened to be women's work.

Their scrutiny was thorough. They prodded Mutton Chop, raised his limbs, thumbed his eyelids open, called at him, laid ears against his bloodied chest, pinched and slapped at him. Farthing lifted his foot and, after a nod from Mama, bit deep into the meat of his big toe. The pain test, Pearl realised. If incisors sunk clear through to the bone didn't wake him—

Dropping the foot and backing away, Farthing began to keen. Mama joined in. Silver and One-Eye lifted their faces and howled. Bluey howled too. The noise was tremendous. Pearl clamped both hands over her ears. Distressed, Titch rolled about in the dirt, yowling. Bubs detached from the nipple and wailed.

Pearl would go *mad* from this noise. Would yield what little scrap of mind she had left.

Her voice lost, she sobbed, "Help me. Oh, won't somebody help me—"

A familiar note in the cacophony jolted her into an alarmed and watchful silence. She sat up. Held her breath. No. It couldn't be. Out here in the wilderness, miles from civilisation? Impossible. She was hearing things. Why, it had sounded like... Or had it? Pearl strained her ears, trying to listen through the tones of rowdy discord.

There.

Unmistakable! Another bark! Pearl leaned over the balcony of Bluey's cupped hands and gazed frantically about the bush until she saw—

Dot!

The scruffy terrier was peeking out from behind a low-lying banksia, dithering on all four paws in a state of anxious indecision; darting forward a few inches, darting back. Dot feared the Yahoo-Devil-Devils with good reason. Pearl's imagination saw Dot fall from giant fingers like a peanut into a gaping mouth, and her heart jangled wildly in panic.

"Stay!" Pearl screamed. "Stay!"

Obediently, Dot lay down on her stomach. Yet she licked her chops and drummed her front paws, clearly agitated, wishing to rush to Pearl's side. Good God! Had Dot run all the way from the Smiths' station, for hours and hours? No, no… Of course not. The dog was fresh and full of pep. Dot had travelled into these mountains via some conveyance, perhaps a horse or…or *a motorcar.*

Pearl wiped away tears. Eddie had come for her. Eddie was somewhere nearby. Soon, her ordeal would be over. The Yahoo-Devil-Devils brayed and bawled. Pearl kept shouting, "Stay! Stay!" To lose Dot would be more than she could possibly bear.

***

From the ridge, they watched Dot scamper across the bowl of the valley towards the bush where the Yahoo-Devil-Devils might have their lair. Eddie felt a terrible panic.

"Shouldn't we go after her?" he said.

"After a *dog*?" the rider scoffed. "Nah. Fuck that for a joke."

Mavis put her hand on Eddie's shoulder. "She'll be right. Animal instincts and all that."

Jack added, "It's a good sign, I reckon. Shows that Pearl's alive."

"And Big Stanley too," Mavis said.

Jack nodded. "Uh, yeah. Big Stanley too."

Dot disappeared into the bush. Agitated, Eddie felt a mounting unease. This rider from the station, this *stranger,* wanted them to stay put, do nothing, and wait for the posse. But for how long? Pearl was close. Why couldn't they charge like Dot? They were armed, weren't they?

The rider took off his hat, dismounted and threw the reins over the nearest tree branch. Snorting, the horse bent its head and cropped at the meagre grass.

"Got any water?" the rider said.

Jack gave him a bottle, and he drank greedily.

"What's your name, kid?" Mavis said.

"Roy Wilkes. I'm one of the Smiths' drovers." He handed back the bottle, wavered, sat down suddenly in the dirt and closed his eyes. Grimacing, he dug his fingers into his eyelids. "Aw, what the hell am I doing here?"

"Trying to save a few lives," Jack said. "Same as us."

"Those monsters just killed my cousin. Right there in front of me. Bit him almost in half. We were shooting and they… He got knocked down, picked up, bitten. Thrown into the scrub like rubbish. How am I gonna tell Mum? Auntie Jean?"

Mavis patted his back. “It’s a bloody nightmare, kid. For all of us.”

“And Alfred?” he continued, as if not hearing. “You see him get drug behind his horse?”

“Yeah,” Jack muttered. “We saw.”

Roy Wilkes began to cry. “Alfred was my best mate. We’ve driven sheep and cattle together for years, from one end of Victoria to the other. Even into New South Wales this one time...” He gave a weak chuckle. “Alf can play harmonica like nobody’s business. Not just bush music neither. All that classical shit, like…like Brahms’s lullaby, for instance. At night, we’d sit around the campfire—” Wilkes sobbed openly in huge, gulping gasps.

“We’re really sorry,” Mavis said.

“Hey,” Jack said. “We’ve got some grub with us. You want something to eat?”

“And that fucker, George!” Wilkes yelled, startling them all. “The gutless wonder! We’re halfway up this hill, galloping towards perdition, and he goes, ‘My horse doesn’t like the smell. I’m heading back to the station.’ Doesn’t like the *smell*?” Wilkes screwed up his nose in disbelief. “If I ever see that son of a bitch again, I’ll break his skull.”

Eddie said, “We actually met him. Crossed paths on our way up here.”

“We sussed him straight away as a quitter,” Mavis said.

“Here you go, mate,” Jack said, coming back from the car and holding out a tin with its own built-in key. “Ham if you’re peckish. There’s whiskey too.”

In a paroxysm of sudden fury, Wilkes scrubbed both forearm sleeves across his dirty, tear-stained face and stared about at them, eyes glittering. “I’ll tell you what and you can mark my words,” he said through gritted teeth, “first chance I get, I’m shooting those Yahoos.

Shooting them dead and straight to the devil. You got ammunition to spare?"

Eddie didn't like the crazed look in this young man's eyes, but Mavis said, "Yeah, we can share ammo."

"I'll kill 'em," Wilkes muttered, gazing at the dirt. "Just watch me. Every last one."

Eddie, exchanging worried glances with Jack and Mavis, said, "Give him whiskey."

Jack nodded, went to the supplies and found a bottle. Meanwhile, Eddie and Mavis moved to the other side of the Model T and conferred in low voices.

"What should we do now?" Eddie asked.

"I don't know. Extra men would sure come in handy."

"Wait for the posse? Come on, Mavis. You want to sit here and twiddle our thumbs?"

"Well, how long do you reckon it'd take Mrs Smith to gather a posse and bring it here?"

"How long?" Eddie sneered. "How long is a piece of string? Nah, the question is: are we gonna keep waiting or not? Pearl is down there. And Big Stanley too. They're already in danger. Are we gonna put up our feet for a cavalry that might never arrive?"

Mavis, perplexed, shook her head in nervous indecision.

Eddie said, "Jesus, even Dot the terrier has more balls than us!"

Hopper made a leisurely approach, lolloping on hind legs, chewing grass with his snout quivering. They both turned to him. Mavis reached out a hand, but Hopper ducked it as Eddie knew he would. The only person that Hopper allowed to touch him was Big Stanley.

"Dot ran into the valley after Pearl," Mavis whispered. "Why didn't Hopper follow?"

Eddie pulled at his earlobe. "Kangaroos aren't like dogs, I guess. No sense of smell."

She regarded him with mournful eyes. "About five years back, Taylor's Travelling Troupe was up north.

One night, me and Big Stanley decided to walk to the nearest pub for a drink. Something other than beer or whiskey, right? Alongside the road was a dead kangaroo. Must've been hit by a car. But its gut was moving. Turns out the movement was a joey still in the pouch. With its mum dead, the poor little bugger didn't stand a chance. Sad, but that's life. I said, 'C'mon, let's go'. Big Stanley ignored me. He tucked the joey into his shirt, named it Hopper on the fucken spot, and looked after him from that day forward. Hand fed him with a baby bottle all hours of the day and night till Hopper could forage for himself." Mavis tried to smile. "His whole life long, Hopper has reckoned Big Stanley as his mother. So, I ask you again: why the fuck didn't Hopper follow Dot into the valley?"

Eddie stared at Mavis with tears filling his eyes.

***

Dot's paws stammered against the ground. The terrier was wound up, excited, as if waiting for a ball to be thrown.

Desperately, Pearl kept shouting, "Stay! Stay!"

Could Dot hear over the cacophony of keening wails? Maybe not. Yet surely, a dog would have enough sense and instinct to be afraid of such beasts, to keep out of their sight—

As if on cue, the howling Yahoo-Devil-Devil clan fell silent. The abrupt quiet gave Pearl a momentary sensation of vertigo. The females stepped back. Silver and One-Eye took hold of Mutton Chop's wrists and began to drag him from the clearing. Where were they taking him? Pearl could only imagine. Grandma had told her once that elephants in Africa make graveyards for their dead kin. Perhaps Yahoo-Devil-Devils had the same practice. She gazed up at Bluey, but his stoic chin didn't give anything away.

Once Mutton Chop's body disappeared into the scrub, Mama and Farthing began to talk in their strange language. Titch and Bubs remained mute. Bluey too. Pearl was sure now that Bluey must be aged somewhere between dependent child and autonomous adult, which meant he fitted in nowhere. Pearl remembered what that had felt like. Remembered her mother's coldness, her grandmother's lack of care and respect. Sniffing back tears, she looked towards the banksia tree for the comforting sight of Dot. The terrier was gone.

Panic speared through Pearl's chest. "Dot!" she called. "Where are you? Dot!"

No sign. As if the dog had never been there at all.

Pearl put palms to her temples and squeezed. Hallucinating. She must be hallucinating and going crazy. From thirst, if nothing else. What other explanation could there be?

Silver's long, one-note roar echoed across the bushland.

As if summoned, the Yahoo-Devil-Devils got up and started walking through the trees towards his call. Now what? Clearly, whatever was to happen next must have something to do with Mutton Chop's corpse. They weren't finished with him yet... Oh God, was Pearl about to witness a cannibalistic feast? She shivered in fear and revulsion.

Soon, the burbling chatter of the river came to her ears. *Water*. Just the thought of it seemed to further shrivel her dry throat and swell her tongue, pound her headache.

They came to the river and stopped.

Mutton Chop was at the water's edge, arranged supine, his chest and belly festooned with scores of red blossoms. Silver and One-Eye had stripped dozens of branches from bottlebrush trees and laid them over him like some kind of funereal wreath. The sight was oddly moving. She recalled her grandmother's coffin; from the garden, a young Pearl had picked a bouquet of blue hydrangeas, tied it with kitchen string, and laid it on the lid.

She expected more wails and screams from the clan, but the silence continued. The beasts solemnly regarded Mutton Chop for a time. Then Silver and One-Eye pushed his body into the water. The current took it. For a few seconds, Mutton Chop remained on his back. Slowly, as if rolling over in bed, he tipped face-down. The bottlebrush branches floated to the surface, creating a ring of flowers about him. His legs dipped under the surface. Soon, he would sink altogether. The current carried him around the bend of the river, and he was gone.

8.

Silver strode into the river. One-Eye followed. Once they were both knee-high, they faced the bank. The remaining clan waded in to join them. As Bluey entered the water, two conflicting, desperate and equally powerful emotions consumed Pearl: the need for a drink versus the fear of drowning. Then she leaned over, reaching for the river. The need for a drink had won.

Each grown Yahoo-Devil-Devil cupped water into a hand and slurped. Mama offered her palm to Titch, who was propped on her hip. Similarly, Farthing gave sips to Bubs. This must be part of the funeral ceremony. Parched, dry lips scabbed, Pearl watched Bluey guzzle water until she cracked.

"Hey!" she yelled.

Surprised, he looked on her expectantly.

"What about *me*?" she said, violently gesturing towards herself.

But he frowned, mystified. He didn't understand! Emphatically, over and over, she pointed at the water with one hand and at her mouth with the other. *Please* let him understand. How could he not realise that, as a living thing, she needed water? She felt like a bug caught in a jar by an uncomprehending child. Or like that kitten killed by the rough play of a toddler who didn't know any better. Oh, dear God—

Comprehension flashed in his eyes at last! She could have wept.

Bluey gave out a sharp bark. The others paused to give attention. He made a great show of dipping his hand into the river and presenting his cupped palm to Pearl. She eagerly began to quaff great draughts of the precious liquid. Wet, cool, wonderful. Relief almost made her swoon. The river tasted earthy and green with an astringency reminiscent of black unsweetened tea. It was the most delicious drink she had ever tasted in her life. When Bluey went to retract his hand, she wrapped an arm about his pinky and kept drinking. He laughed. The others did too, quietly and lightly. She kept drinking until she couldn't hold any more, until the weight of her distended stomach sat heavy in her guts like a bowling ball. Finally replete, she lifted her face, gasping.

Bluey kissed her crown and gazed at her with fondness, tickling under her chin. She glanced around. The rest of the clan were looking at her with kind and friendly faces – even Silver. For a moment, their change of heart felt confusing. Until she realised that drinking from the river after Mutton Chop's funeral must be a sign of respect for the dead. By accident, she had aligned herself with the clan. Now she was safe.

Safe!

Laughing and sobbing, she beamed about at them. They smiled back. Safe! Tonight, while everyone slept, she would creep away and run towards the Smiths' station. She just needed to get her bearings first. The setting sun would point her east. Safe!

Oh, she was safe!

The rapid draining away of intense stress weakened her with the speed of an injected soporific. Exhausted, she drooped in Bluey's hand. Her eyes closed. She heard and felt his exit from the river. The others splashed around him. Pearl's last conscious thought was that the clan must be heading to the clearing. Then she fell into a soft, easy and dreamless sleep.

***

Roy Wilkes forked the last of the ham into his mouth, dropped the can to the ground and stood up. "Okay, let's ride," he said. "The posse ain't coming. Who's with me?"

"I am," Eddie said, relieved to be doing something, *anything*, to rescue Pearl.

Jack said, "We need more men. No way we can kill those monsters by ourselves—"

"Bullshit, we can't." Wilkes grinned with clenched teeth. "Me, Norman and Alf shot to death at least one of the pricks. We've got enough fire power. There's only three more!"

"Just three more that we *saw*," Mavis pointed out. "There could be a mob in reserve."

Wilkes laughed. "Three, ten, fifty, a hundred of the fuckers – I don't give a goddamn."

Wasn't his rifle empty? His saddlebags bereft of ammunition? He seemed prepared to charge into the clan's lair without any means of self-defence. Such foolhardiness sent a chill through Eddie. Distraught and grieving, Wilkes was in no fit state to make decisions. But Pearl was so alone, so vulnerable, in such awful peril and desperate for rescue—

"Okay, we're all going," Eddie said.

Jack and Mavis didn't object. The next ten minutes passed in a frenzy of preparation.

"Do we take the car or not?" Mavis said. "It's fucken noisy. They'll hear us coming."

"It's either that or travel by foot," Jack said. "How do we make a quick escape on foot?"

They both regarded Eddie for an answer. Such deference surprised him since he was the youngest. Then again, he was only one who knew how to drive. That skill held weight.

At last, he said, “All right, we take the car. Speed is more important than stealth.”

Chuckling, his smile spasmodically twitching in tic after nervous tic, Wilkes went around and grabbed everyone by the hand one at a time, shaking vigorously. “We’ll be brothers in arms,” he said gaily, his voice affecting a sing-song cadence. “Brothers in blood. Kill or be killed. One way in and one way out.”

“Mate, are you okay?” Eddie said.

Wilkes ran to his horse. With a practised leap that put one foot unerringly in the stirrup, he swung onto the saddle, grabbed the reins and pulled his horse’s head towards the valley. “Home or hell,” he shouted gleefully. “I’ll see you bitches again somewhere.” Lifting his loaded rifle, he dug his spurs. The horse bunched its haunches and bolted down the incline, raising great clouds of dust.

Mavis whistled and said, “The poor kid’s lost his fucken mind.”

“As mad as a gum tree of galahs,” Jack agreed. “He’ll shoot anything that moves.”

In a sudden accord, they exchanged frightened glances.

“Get in the car,” Eddie ordered, heading for the driver’s door. “Let’s go, c’mon. Let’s go!”

***

The familiar noise broke into Pearl’s dreams. Be quiet, she thought crossly. It’s too early. She felt cosy in bed, warm and comfortable with the blankets tucked to her chin, and had no desire to get up. Yet Dot wouldn’t stop barking. The terrier must want her breakfast. With reluctance, loath to leave her slumber, Pearl stretched, yawned and opened her eyes.

To a canopy of eucalyptus trees.

The cup of Bluey's hand.

A late morning in the bush that held a clan of Yahoo-Devil-Devils munching on leaves.

Startled, Pearl sat up, heart drumming. After the earlier hallucination, had she now *dreamt* the sounds of Dot's bark? Of course, yes, she *must* have dreamt it. Surely, Dot couldn't possibly have run all the way—

No! There it was again!

But how could Dot, Pearl's constant and faithful companion since Grandma's funeral, be out here in the middle of Woop Woop? Pearl gaped around in a wild and frightened state. And God, she wasn't the only one scanning: the clan had stopped eating, each member turning their head this way and that to locate the source of the noise. Oh, how they might relish a snack of fresh dog meat for lunch—

"Stay!" Pearl cried in desperation. "Wherever you are, stay! Stay!"

She saw Dot peeking out from behind a nearby tree. As they locked eyes, Dot stopped barking and, excited, hung out her tongue, tail wagging. The sight brought a sting of tears and a flush of hopeless resignation, for Pearl knew that Dot was now as good as dead.

"Won't you please go," she murmured, vision blurring. "Please run away."

The dog trotted from behind the tree as if blind to the Yahoo-Devil-Devils, her long red tongue bobbing out of a huge grin. Pearl's heart constricted into a ball.

Bubs noticed Dot first, extending a hairy arm to point, making an excited *mmm-mmm* sound. The others watched the terrier's progress across the clearing with amazement. Why did they seem so baffled? Then Pearl realised that, of course, they were used to the wild dingo. How very different the terrier looked! The dingo was a large, dog-like wolf with a barrel chest and short reddish coat, whereas Dot was small enough to sit in a hat, and her sand-coloured fur was long and silky. These beasts wouldn't know what to make of her.

Perhaps that was Dot's saving grace: too unusual to risk eating…?

No. Pearl was fooling herself and she knew it. Her eyes filled with tears.

"Run," she whispered helplessly. "Please go. Dot, run away."

Titch, taking the finger out of his nose, moved as if to intercept the dog.

However, Bluey shuffled forward and put his free hand to the ground. Either due to familiarity with the beast or because of Pearl, Dot headed for Bluey's palm. With a delicate hop, she alighted. Weeping in terror, Pearl reached out. Bluey tipped Dot into Pearl's arms. She embraced Dot tightly. Oh God, the beloved smell of her fur, the familiar feel of her warm, wriggling body… Pearl buried her face against Dot and cried in desperation and grief. The terrier lapped at her tears. Bluey touched his forefinger along them both, crooning.

"My darling sweetie," Pearl sobbed. "My dearest, darling sweetie. How did you get here? How on earth did you find me?"

Bubs wouldn't stop pointing at Dot and making keen *mmm-mmm* exclamations. Finally, he pushed away from Farthing and tumbled from her grasp. Crawled over the ground towards them, getting nearer, nearer... Farthing and the other Yahoo-Devil-Devils did nothing to stop him. Pearl watched his advance with dread. Close now, too close, Bubs extended a finger to the cup of Bluey's hand to point at Dot. He scooched even closer, turned up his small, eager face to Bluey and made questioning *huh-huh-huh* sounds. Bluey harrumphed. What could that *harrumph* possibly mean? Pearl hugged Dot to her chest and turned away. Like a traitor – or an *idiot* – the terrier squirmed free to sniff and lick at Bubs' exploratory finger.

Panic rising, Pearl snapped, "Bad dog! Stop that! Stop it, I tell you!"

Any second now, Bubs would haul out Dot and kill her. Any second now. By accident or design, it didn't matter. Any second now…

The seconds ticked on.

Pearl released her breath and sucked in another. Meanwhile, Bubs patted Dot gently, reverently. Dot kept licking Bubs' finger. It began to dawn on Pearl that perhaps the worst wouldn't happen. Bubs *wasn't* about to kill Dot. The other Yahoo-Devil-Devils watched the interaction with kind, indulgent expressions. Bubs puckered his lips and made kissing noises. Goodness, he seemed quite taken with the terrier. Must think her the bee's knees. It hardly seemed possible…

"We're safe," Pearl marvelled to Dot at last. "My God, we're both safe."

On impulse, she reached out and stroked Bubs' head. The strawberry-blonde hair felt coarse like twine. Bubs looked at Pearl, his enormous blue eyes fringed with dark lashes, and smiled. Why, he had only four blunt teeth; two on the top and two on the bottom, like a human infant. Pearl couldn't help smiling in return.

"Aren't you lovely?" she said, caressing Bubs' cheek. "Oh, you're such a cutie."

Bluey hooted quietly. The other members of the clan shuffled forward, crowding around to get a better look. Pearl gazed up at the ring of monstrous, simian faces and long, yellowed fangs, and saw tenderness in their expressions.

Turning his full attention now to Pearl, Bubs fingered a tress of her hair, inspected it closely and sniffed it. Curiosity satisfied, he laid the tress carefully on her shoulder and smoothed it down with a light tap. He held out a hank of his own forearm hair and burped.

"Yes, I'm blonde just like you," she said, and dutifully fondled the hank.

With a giggle, he pushed away to roll about in the dirt, holding both his feet, until he came to a stop near Titch and sat up. Bubs' taunting raspberry seemed to say: *Ha, Titch, I'm allowed to touch Bluey's pet and you're not!* Titch scowled and, as if consoling himself, dug for gold in his nose.

There was nothing to fear!

Tonight, when the Yahoo-Devil-Devils fell asleep, she would simply head east with Dot. The ordeal would be over. Pearl might suffer nightmares for a time, naturally – of the Yahoo-Devil-Devil attack on the Smiths' station; Tom's horrible death; the dismemberments of Big Stanley, Mr Smith, the worker unfolding like a pamphlet – but no, no, surely the distressing dreams would pass if she put her mind to it. Filled her life with good, kind things. Happy things. And refused to dwell – *wallow* – in the past. Unlike Mum, she wouldn't use gin to blot out bad memories. Would she? Of course not. Pearl was made of stronger stuff than her mother. Wasn't she? Yes. As long as she had Dot. And maybe Eddie...

"I'll be leaving soon," Pearl told Bluey. "You know, I think I'll miss you. Just a smidge."

Bluey touched her face with a light forefinger. She turned her cheek into it.

The clan broke away and duckwalked back towards the bushes, whereupon they recommenced stripping branches to munch at blooms and leaves. A handful of rainbow lorikeets fossicked in one of the nearby gum trees, the colourful birds jumping from bough to bough and even hanging upside-down to nibble at the trailing blossoms. They didn't seem afraid of the Yahoo-Devil-Devils in the slightest. The beasts mustn't hunt or eat birds. Pearl watched the lorikeets as they fed, admiring their bright red beaks, their vibrant purple and green plumage. Bluey offered a flowering stem and Pearl took it graciously.

"Thank you," she said with a sigh. "Well, anyhow, I guess it's the thought that counts."

Her stomach grumbled. As soon as she was back in the Smiths' kitchen, she would *eat* and *eat*. First, a buttery fried egg on a toasted sandwich – with bacon if Mrs Smith had a spare rasher. Followed by a stroll through the back yard to pluck apples and oranges off the trees, and strawberries from the planter boxes. Oh, she could almost taste the juicy sweetness! And poor starving Dot would have a huge bowl of mince—

Pearl broke from her indulgent reverie. Studied Dot. The dog's clear, bright eyes stared back, and her coat looked brushed and clean. No, Dot wasn't hungry at all, hadn't run for hours and hours up this mountain. No, someone had brought her. Once again, Pearl's thoughts flew to Eddie. He was here. *He was here!* And then a tremor of anxiety tightened her chest. Pearl didn't need to be rescued anymore. If Eddie burst into the clearing now with guns blazing—

A faint sound came to her ears.

What was it? Breath held, she waited as the sound came closer: the slow, measured, rhythmic four-beat crush of leaf litter. *A horse*. The clan hadn't noticed. It must be one of the riders who had shot and killed Mutton Chop coming back to finish the job.

"Rider!" she called out. "Turn back! I'm okay. There's no need to risk your life. Once the beasts are asleep, I'll escape. Rider! Turn back while you still can."

Bluey stopped chewing to tickle beneath her chin. She looked up at his enquiring face. Clearly, he wondered why she was shouting when lunch was supposed to be a quiet time.

"Don't worry," she said, patting his thumb, putting on a smile.

Appeased, Bluey popped another blossom into his mouth. The clan had started their odd humming again. However, it wasn't the same song of contentment they had sung earlier at breakfast. No, this was mournful, a dirge for the passing of Mutton Chop. Preoccupied by grief…that was why they hadn't noticed the sound of horse's hooves. Oh, just the thought of Bluey getting shot again – Pearl stiffened at the sight of his gunshot wound. God, the state of it! Weeping a thin, clear and oily fluid. Soon, that fluid would be thick and yellow. Infection! If his body couldn't fight it off, he risked blood poisoning and death. Now, an armed rider was lurking nearby with a rifle, planning to shoot Bluey again.

"Go away!" Pearl shouted. "There's no need to shoot! Go away!"

Excited, Dot squirmed and barked.

"Hush," Pearl cried, trying to hold the dog still. "Be quiet so I can listen if the horse—"

She gasped. Another sound, getting nearer. A thrumming, continuous, mechanical noise.

A car. The Model T! Her flirty conversation with Eddie rushed back…

Are those eyes on the front of it? The two round things on its muzzle?

Those round things are lights. You switch them on to see where you're going in the dark. And it's not a 'muzzle' but a compartment called a bonnet. Inside is the engine.

The Model T's engine droned. The Yahoo-Devil-Devils paid no attention, perhaps assuming it was something natural like a swarm of bees. Pearl felt faint. No, Eddie, no…

The abrupt sound of galloping made the clan scramble to sit up. Silver and One-Eye jumped to their feet, showing teeth. Bluey moved back, enclosing Pearl and Dot in the cup of his hands. Breathless, Pearl peeked over his fingers.

A man on a horse stopped at the clearing's edge. He sighted along a rifle.

***

"It's too fucken steep," Mavis argued from the back seat. "No way. Are we really gonna try this stunt? We'll go arse over tit. We ought to find a safer route into the valley."

"That'd take ages," Jack said, "Besides, Eddie knows what he's doing."

No, he didn't.

Eddie could drive as well as anybody on sealed or dirt roads, sure, yet this mountainous decline was something else. If he pranged the car like Mavis predicted, what would happen to them? To Pearl? But if he stayed put, too scared to move…? Gritting his teeth, Eddie eased the Model T over the lip of the ridge. The sky seemed to teeter in the windscreen. Here goes nothing, he thought, and pressed a little harder on the pedal. The car lurched forward.

Then – *thump* – dropped over.

And found no traction at all.

The car skated and slid crazily down the hill. Eddie steered as best he could between trees. Bushes got run over. Ground animals scattered. Squawking, birds flew off. A branch knocked out a headlight with a smash of holophane glass. Tyres bounced over rocks. Supplies tumbled about inside the cabin. Eddie kept losing his seat. Mavis and Jack hung on for dear life. Sweat broke across Eddie's back. The skinny tyres couldn't find purchase in the dirt. Christ, the car was starting to *bounce*, higher and higher. In the next few seconds, they would turn over— The hillside levelled out a fraction. Not much, but enough.

Wrestling the steering wheel, Eddie regained control of the Model T.

Mavis patted his shoulder. "Well, it's a good thing I ain't got dentures," she said, voice hoarse, "because I would've swallowed them."

"You ought to be one of them racing drivers," Jack said. "Good job, mate."

More like good luck. If they only knew...but Eddie said nothing. He glanced out the rear window. There was Hopper, following in their wake. Hopper must consider the workers of Taylor's Travelling Troupe as his family. If the worst came to the worst and its 'family' was wiped out, would the kangaroo be able to survive in the wild, join a mob of its own kind? Eddie shivered. He wondered what had happened to Dot. And where in God's name was Wilkes? There had been no gunshots. Shit, was Mrs Smith's posse on its way or not? The weight of so much *not knowing* constricted Eddie's ribcage and cramped his lungs.

They reached the valley floor. Pressing the pedal, he sped across the hard-packed earth. The brown and lazy river burbled on his left. The tyres ran over patches of dried blood, yet Eddie couldn't think about that right now. Dead ahead, across the flat expanse speckled with grasses, stood a wide bank of trees and bushes, the spot where Jack assumed the monsters' lair must be hidden. Anxiety tingled in Eddie's fingertips and toes.

"Listen," he said, "when we get there, I'm gonna leave the engine running and in gear. If something happens to me, you aim where you want to go by moving this here steering wheel from side to side, you see how I'm doing it now, and plant your foot on—"

Mavis slapped the back of his head.

"Ow!" Eddie said. "What the hell was that for?"

"Don't invite bad luck. Quit flapping your gums about it."

"We'll be fine," Jack said. "We've got rifles, haven't we?"

So had the horsemen from the Smiths' station, Eddie thought, and look what happened to *them*. Again, he chose to stay silent. They were all frightened to death. No point in harping.

He slowed to a putter. Ahead, the gum trees were large and tall, maybe thirty feet high apiece, with plenty of ground between them. Only scrappy shrubs and herbage had managed to grow beneath the shade of their overarching canopy. Enough room for the passage of Yahoo-Devil-Devils; more than enough room for a Model T. Nonetheless, he braked.

"What's the matter?" Jack said.

"I don't know if I should drive straight in there. We need an element of surprise, right? Otherwise, they'll just see us and attack. Maybe it'd be smarter if I circled round."

Mavis said, "But we don't know if their hangout is straight on or not. Maybe it's somewhere along this time-wasting circuit you wanna do."

"She's right," Jack said. "We've got no idea which way is safest, so let's keep going."

Eddie bit his lip. "Should we try to scout the area first?"

"What for?" Mavis said.

"Well, for starters, we can't rescue anybody if we get ourselves killed," he retorted.

"Scout it how?" She waved a dismissive hand. "No matter what kind of stuffing about we choose, the monsters will hear the car and come investigate. Full steam ahead, driver."

Jack said, "All right, Mavis, let's ready the guns."

Eddie released the brake and pressed the pedal. Through the seat, he felt the chuckling thrum of the engine. This might be one of the last sensations he would ever experience – apart from the pain of a horrible death. The forest ahead lay dim and quiet. To give himself strength, Eddie brought to mind Pearl's face: big hazel eyes, pure white skin, pinched little mouth as red as a cherry. Remembered their drive into town for supplies, and how she had worn her oversized straw hat jammed low to stop her golden hair from flying about. Remembered how much he admired her outlook, resilience, attitude. How much he loved her from the first moment he had laid eyes on her.

Only a few days ago, when the troupe had had their tent smack-bang in the middle of the town's agricultural show, Eddie had been sitting around after lunch with a mug of coffee when he'd spotted Big Stanley leading a stranger with a suitcase from the Taylors' caravan.

"And here's our driver, car mechanic and roustabout, Eddie Clark," Big Stanley said.

Eddie politely stood up. Gee, this girl was *short*. When she took off her hat, Eddie gazed upon the prettiest face he'd ever seen. His expression must have been revealing, for she blushed and looked down demurely for a moment, her lashes fanning.

"This is Miss Bennett, our new cook and bottle-washer," Big Stanley said.

"Oh please, call me Pearl," she said, and held out her hand.

Eddie took it. So small and fine-boned, yet callused, used to hard work. And her dress, although clean, was threadbare; the suitcase made from cardboard. Just another young kid without family or luck, same as Eddie, but with such a confident and cheerful air. He had felt a desire to look after her, to cherish her, even before he had spoken a single word in reply—

"Mate, here you go," Jack said, passing over a rifle into the front seat.

Eddie put the rifle across his lap. Touched at Tom's loaded revolver at his waistband. Tightened his grip on the steering wheel. Pushed down on the accelerator.

They entered the shadowed forest.

9.

Nervous, the horse nickered. The barrel of the rifle loomed black. The rider had dark hair covered in red dust. Pearl could see his watering eyes, shaking hands, trembling mouth.

"Stop!" she yelled. "Stop! Don't shoot!"

Bang. An orange explosion flowered from the barrel.

Farthing shrieked and fell back. Was she wounded? Or just startled?

Dot barked hysterically. The Yahoo-Devil-Devils jumped up, spun about in screeching alarm, confused. The rider loaded, steered the horse through the clearing to reveal himself, shot again single-handed. The clan scattered. Silver and One-Eye raced towards the threat. Bellowing, they swung their arms. The horse, bucking and snorting, ducked away and threaded through a narrow grouping of trees where Yahoo-Devil-Devils couldn't follow. Pearl heard the *click* of the rider opening the Martini-Henry's breech.

"There's no need to shoot them!" she cried. "Please! I'll escape at night!"

Mama and Farthing, clutching their children, fled. Bluey stood up, dithered. Would he follow the males or the females? Dot leapt out of his hands.

“Dot!” Pearl cried. “No! Come back!”

Another shot. More growling.

Pearl found herself crying in panic, but for who or what, she was no longer sure.

***

A gunshot sounded. Eddie’s nervous system crackled with adrenaline. Reflexively, he stamped the accelerator flat. The car flew. Tore between gum trees. Shadows and light flickered staccato from overhead. Yahoo-Devil-Devils roared. Another gunshot echoed around the mountains. The battle sounded nearby. Eddie ought to slow down.

“Fucken hell,” Mavis gasped. “This is it. Do or die.”

Eddie squeezed the steering wheel in his fists. Pearl! He was so close to rescuing her.

The thick cluster of forest abruptly ended. The Model T careered into an open clearing. Eddie wrenched the wheel to avoid smashing into the heels of Yahoo-Devil-Devils. One beast looked around, noticed the Model T, and squinted its solitary eye, baring teeth.

“Back up!” Mavis yelled. “Hurry!”

Eddie stamped the reverse pedal, threw his free arm over the seat and looked out the rear window, aiming between trees. Hopper bounded away. The engine whined at a fever pitch. Growling, the one-eyed bastard stamped in pursuit, shaking the ground. Even in his panic, Eddie’s blood grew hot. This was the Yahoo that had killed Tom, and Eddie wanted to shoot the son-of-a-bitch right in its ugly face.

“Jesus *Christ*!” Mavis shouted.

“Faster!” Jack yelled.

The car lifted. Eddie thought he’d bumped over a rock or tree root, and wrestled with the steering wheel to regain control with no effect. Mavis and Jack were screaming. In confused consternation, Eddie worked the steering and levers until the ground dropped away, and he understood what had happened: the monster had picked up the Model T in both giant hands.

The bloodshot eye glared through the windscreen.

God, the stink of rotten eggs steaming from its fur, that sour and fishy breath—

Snarling, the monster dropped the car to the ground. Eddie's body slammed. Metal crunched. Glass broke. The car bounced once, then rolled. A hard knock against Eddie's head swirled the world, for how long he couldn't tell. He watched supplies toss inside the cabin; the tumbling movements of Jack and Mavis, their limbs loose and boneless. He assumed his own body must be somersaulting too, colliding with fixed and free objects, even though, somehow, he couldn't feel a thing. The car came to a wrenching stop.

Upside down, against a tree.

The engine was still running. Wheels squeaked and rattled as they continued to turn.

Dirt drifted throughout the cabin. Eddie lay where the prang had put him, dazed but coming back to himself, tentatively feeling himself to be alive. There was pain in his knee and wrist, a knot on his head. Gingerly, he tested his body. Found he could move all right. He pushed tin cans and bottles from his chest, and gazed about. There was Jack. And there was Mavis. Both stirring. Thank Christ. Eddie struggled to sit up.

A giant hand grabbed the car, throwing it about.

Eddie toppled headfirst into the passenger-side footwell. He felt his nose break. Something heavy landed on his legs momentarily and rolled away.

Screeching, a corner of the roof peeled back.

The scarred and one-eyed face leered down. Finding himself the right way up, Eddie groped for a rifle. Found one. Aimed. Pulled the trigger. A hole exploded in the monster's cheek, and a mist of hot blood sprayed over Eddie's face. He fumbled for another cartridge and was suddenly compressed against the seat as the car lifted at great speed. Then he was pitched – along with Mavis, Jack and every object not pinned down – to one side as the car arced through the air. The bastard had thrown it! A blurring whip of leaves whizzed past as the Model T sailed. Surely, they would hit a tree and be dashed to pieces. The car reached the peak of its parabola and began to drop. Everything inside it became weightless.

Falling seemed to take a long time.

The Model T skidded and skipped along the ground, rolled, and stuttered to a halt. The world went away. It returned through a red mist. Eddie wiped a forearm across his eyes to clear the blood. More blood ran into his eyes. He explored his face with shaking hands. There, a deep gash on his forehead. Coughing, he spat more blood and a few teeth. *Where was he?* What on God's green earth had just happened? He must have been caught playing the shell game again, been cornered in a laneway by some Melbourne coppers armed with cudgels.

Eddie crawled through a window. He recognised sunshine as he dropped onto his back and lay there, panting, staring through a leafy canopy at a blue sky dotted by white, wispy clouds. It looked to be a fine morning with the fresh and flowery smell of early spring.

Above him, a giant paw.

Christ! The paw reaching down. A woman's full-throated scream.

Eddie came immediately to his senses. The one-eyed bastard, rummaging through the ruined car, was grabbing hold of Mavis. Lifting her towards its mouth, ready for the bite. Yet she had a rifle. Her shot blew off a chunk of its eyebrow. Reprieve! Howling, the monster swung its head, the tattered skin showering gore.

Scrambling in the wreckage, Eddie found a rifle and shot the monster again. A section of its belly hair puffed and showed blood.

"Jack!" Eddie yelled. "Jack, you gotta help us! Jack?"

No answer.

Eddie dug and found a box of cartridges. Fingers trembling, he shoved a cartridge into the breech. Rolled onto his back. Pulled the trigger. Hit the monster in an armpit. Damn. Better than nothing, but Jesus, he had to *aim* next time, try to hit something that mattered.

Recoiling momentarily, the monster snorted, rallied, and shrugged off its injuries. It squinted with malevolent hatred at Mavis, who was kicking hard within its fist, and yawned open its chops. Ropes of saliva stretched between discoloured fangs.

"You lousy *fucker!*" Mavis bellowed.

Swinging her empty rifle like a cricket bat, and with all the strength in her mighty arms, she smashed out one of its teeth.

Eddie cheered. The one-eyed bastard grunted, blood glistening in its mouth. Hot damn, Eddie thought as he reloaded, Mavis would make it out of this fix! She had the gumption! He shot again, this time tufting a hole in the monster's throat, hopefully damaging vital structures. The monster gave an odd, strangling cough.

"We'll get him!" Eddie cried. "Come on, hit him again, Mavis!"

She swung the rifle butt, splitting the simian's lip. Baying, the monster reared up to its full height, hauled back its arm like a fast bowler, and threw Mavis towards the sun. In disbelief, Eddie sat up. He saw Mavis airborne. Flailing, swirling and turning against the backdrop of blue sky and clouds, an ever-dwindling speck.

Then she fell out of sight.

Hiccupping on grief and horror, Eddie grabbed at cartridge boxes, stuffing them in his pockets, inside his shirt. "Jack!" he called, voice breaking. "Jack, for fuck's sake! Jack?"

Why wasn't he answering? Eddie loaded the rifle, screaming through gritted teeth.

Ready, he pointed the barrel. He looked around at nothing but forest. Where was the one-eyed bastard? Gradually, distant sounds came back to Eddie's awareness. Roaring. Shooting. Screaming. *Pearl's screams*. Galvanised, he wobbled to his feet, rifle in hand.

"Eddie?"

He paused, looking back.

Jack, scalp bleeding, gazed through a broken window. "Eddie?" Jack mumbled again, dazed, his jaw hanging at an odd angle. "Are we alive?"

"You and me, yeah. But not Mavis."

"Huh? What do you mean? Is she *dead*?"

"Yeah. I'm off to get Pearl. Stay here. I'll come back for you, okay? Sit tight."

Eddie, limping, raced as fast as he could towards the terrible noises, rifle aimed, heart in his mouth. Trunks, shrubs, bushes, grasses... Suddenly, a clearing. Eddie stopped, gasping.

Wilkes on his wild-eyed horse, which bucked, danced and weaved. Giant monsters swinging and snatching at them.

"*Eddie!*" shrieked a familiar voice. "Eddie, up here! No, higher! *Eddie!*"

Frantic, he gazed into the trees. Clinging to the bough of a eucalypt, mostly obscured by foliage, was Pearl. With a blank smile, she let go and dropped. Eddie's breath seized. No! Would she land and break her legs? Her back? Pearl tumbled into a thick bed of litter. Unsteadily, she gained her feet and staggered towards him, arms outstretched.

Good God!

She was dirty, bruised, bloodied, scabbed, arms and legs scored by countless abrasions, hands and feet cut to pieces, hair knotted and struck through with leaves. Her shredded dress revealed her underwear, belly, the curve of both breasts and a single nipple. She weaved closer.

Purplish contusions lined her chin. One of her eyes was blackened and swollen almost shut. Eddie's heart jangled. What an ordeal she must have suffered! Dropping his rifle, stunned, he opened his arms. She flung herself at him, weeping. They embraced. Christ, he could smell the stink of Yahoo-Devil-Devil on her. Those *bastards*.

Pearl's exhausted body sank, while Eddie did his best to hold her up.

"Oh, I knew you'd come for me," she murmured. "I just knew it…"

"Is there anybody else?"

"No. They killed and ate them all. Mr Smith and his worker… Big Stanley."

Breath catching on a sob, Eddie buried his face in her neck and hugged her tightly. Dot's barking shook him into action. Releasing Pearl and steadying her for a moment by gripping her shoulders, he said, "Hurry, put this on."

He stripped his shirt and helped her thread her hands through the sleeves. The garment hung past her hips. Trembling, she fastened a few buttons which preserved her modesty, then wrapped her arms about him again, surprising him with a kiss on the mouth.

She whispered, "Darling, just let me say—"

"Me too. But we'll talk later, okay?"

She wilted. Eddie reached behind her knees and lifted her into his arms. He lurched away with her. But where was he intending to go? *Where?* The car was smashed beyond repair. Maybe he could get Wilkes' attention somehow, beg Wilkes to spirit Pearl to safety on the back of his horse. Eddie staggered through the bush, Pearl joggling against him, her eyes closed; Dot trotting alongside. They were defenceless. Without a rifle. Oh *shit*, Eddie had cartridges but didn't have the rifle, had forgotten to pick it up—

"Psst! Hey, mate. Over here."

Eddie spun about. He grinned in joy and relief.

Jack was stepping out from behind a gum tree.

He had a bandage wrapped under his chin and knotted on top of his head to keep his busted jaw together, a satchel – presumably filled with supplies – slung over one shoulder, and carried a couple of rifles. Thank Christ, at least Jack was thinking straight. Eddie shuffled over, struggling to support Pearl. Something in his left wrist must be broken.

"I'll swap ya," Jack said. "Here, take the guns. Now, let's go."

"Go? But the car's fucked."

"No, to the river."

Eddie limped after Jack, who was somehow full of beans, dashing through the trees with Pearl in his arms as if she weighed nothing at all. By God, this boxer was so incredibly *fit.* So mentally *tough.* Jack's jaw must be in two or more pieces, yet he wasn't letting the pain slow him down. Inspired, Eddie determined to rise above his own injuries. Broken nose, broken wrist, sprained knee, knocked out teeth, cuts and bruises be *damned.*

He wasn't the only one following Jack. Nearby were Dot and Hopper. A momentary vision of Mavis twirling helplessly through the air crippled Eddie's resolve, but he pushed his sorrow aside and laboured on through the bush. The ground seemed to be dipping. There were more shrubs. The grasses became lusher and greener. He could hear it now, the rippling flow of water. Even the air smelled fresh.

"Hey," he called, "why are we going to the river?"

"To hide our scent," Jack called back.

Hide their *scent*? What the hell did that mean? A quick bath, and then on the run again? Or was Jack expecting them to swim? Mystified, uneasy, Eddie kept running. Would he even remember how to swim? He hadn't been in a body of water larger than a bathtub since he was a kid. Could dogs and kangaroos swim? Behind them, roars and gunshots were fading away as the sound of running water got louder. Then the ground dropped. Eddie skidded down a steep embankment. The river looked wide and brown. Jack was already striding into it.

"Wait a minute!" Eddie called, slipping in the soft mud. "Wait!"

***

Pearl roused as her feet dipped into cold water. She gazed up, expecting Bluey's jutting chin. It was *Jack* holding her in his arms. Dearest Jack! Except he was plunging her into the river.

Sitting up and kicking, she cried, "Stop, no, you'll drown me!"

Jack paused to turn back. There was Eddie, shirtless, his face bloodied, a rifle in either hand. Dot and Hopper waited nearby; ears similarly pricked by tension.

"We either cross the river or die," Jack said. "Eddie, can you swim?"

"I used to sort of dog-paddle—"

"Good enough. Pearl, get behind me. Put your arms around my neck."

Blindly, she obeyed. Jack tipped forward and breast-stroked into the river. Pearl, lying on his back, felt the water's icy embrace and panicked, thrashing in mortal terror.

"Don't choke me!" Jack ordered. "Relax. Close your eyes and relax. Do it or I'll shake you off and let you sink. No, I didn't mean that. Please, trust me, Pearl. You have to *relax*."

Pearl unclenched the tight lock of her arms, put her face on Jack's shoulder and, sobbing, let Fate take over. The water burbled. Gently lifted and drifted her legs. The cool freshness felt like a salve to her bruised body. Jack ploughed across the river. She felt the muscles of his upper back bunching as he breast-stroked. Maybe Pearl wouldn't drown after all. She opened her eyes. Why, they were halfway across. Eddie, holding the rifle barrels in one hand, splashed and kicked and spat water alongside. And Hopper! So, kangaroos could swim—

But where was Dot?

No, no, no, she must be stranded on the other side, too scared to enter the water. Might she escape some other way? Find an overland route to civilisation?

A familiar sneeze turned Pearl's head.

Dot!

Muzzle lifted, eyes intent, the terrier worked her paws in the water, as wilful and determined as ever. Pearl found herself laughing. Jack reached the bank. With his help, Pearl scaled the incline. Dot and Hopper scampered past them to dry land. Last of all struggled Eddie, clawing one-handed through the mud. Pearl reached down and took the rifles for him.

"We made it," she said. "Thank God, everyone's safe."

A wounded expression fleetingly clouded Eddie's face, which she didn't understand.

He blew water and blood from his nostrils. "We've got a long way to run yet. Let's go."

"*Run?*" she said, the full weight of exhaustion hitting her at once. "But didn't you drive?"

"The car got smashed to pieces," Eddie said.

He and Jack took hold of her, an upper arm each, and bolted Pearl into the bush.

Oh, how on earth could she run all the way down this godforsaken mountain? But her bruised feet hardly touched the ground. It felt wondrously like flying. Through the slit of drowsing eyelids, she glimpsed sky and leaves. On the wind, her ears caught the intermittent and faraway sounds of gunshots, growls, neighs, the calls of startled birds. At times, she seemed to dream. When fully awake, she felt the drop of a descent, heard the wheezes of Eddie and Jack, the scampering of Dot and Hopper. They must be heading towards the Smiths' station. Pearl tried to help, tried to run; her feet could neither reach the ground nor keep up. Her bare toes trailed. Nonetheless, she kept a tight hold of both rifles. Only Death itself could prise those barrels from her grip. Images of fried egg sandwiches shimmered in her mind's eye. Baskets of apples, oranges, strawberries. *A proper stove is such a blessing—*

"Look out!" Eddie called.

They stopped. Woozy, Pearl opened her eyes.

Dogs. Six of them. Dogs?

No. A pack of dingoes.

Eddie and Jack released her arms. Pearl sank to the ground. The dingoes approached, snouts retracting, flews peeling back over fangs. Eddie took a revolver from his waistband. Could it fire after getting trawled through the river? She didn't know. The dingoes gnashed their teeth. Oh God, now what?

Hopper leapt high and landed amongst the pack.

Chaos.

The dingoes attacked the kangaroo. Hopper boxed and kicked. The dingoes snapped and lunged. Dot darted at speed into the fray, barking and biting, pulling attention away from Hopper, circling too fast for the dingoes to pursue.

Bang!

Eddie had fired the revolver. A dingo fell back, yelping.

Bang!

Jack pulled a rifle from Pearl's clawed grip.

Bang!

Hopper retreated. A dingo followed. The retreat was a feint; Hopper grabbed the dingo about its neck with both arms and squeezed, chest muscles bunching. The dingo struggled.

Boom!

A different tone of gunshot. Jack must have fired the rifle.

Dot barked on and on, bamboozling the dingoes. Hopper kept strangling. Eddie and Jack kept shooting.

"Give me a gun too!" Pearl cried, faint and cold, trying to stand up. "Let me help."

Eddie leaned a hand towards her. Wavering, warping, he disappeared into a void.

***

She awoke to gentle taps on her cheek, a canteen of water at her lips. Pearl drank. Eddie helped her sit up. Jack was squatting nearby, holding a spoon and an open can of baked beans. Food! He fed her like a baby. After a few delicious mouthfuls, she began to rally. She looked about and saw Dot and Hopper, both unharmed, and felt blessed.

"Oh, where are the dingoes?" she gasped, remembering the attack in sudden terror.

"Gone for now, but they'll be back," Eddie said.

"Pearl, listen to me," Jack said. "Walking out of here will take too long. None of us are in good shape. There's only one way out of this fix and that's to travel by river."

"By river?" Aghast, she pushed the spoon away. "Only if you've got a boat."

Eddie said, "Does the river pass anywhere near your town?"

"It goes right through the middle," she said, "but you can't expect us to swim the whole way. It's too far. We'll surely drown."

Jack smiled. "Not swim: float. The river runs downhill. We just hop in and ride along."

She quailed at the notion of going back into that dark water. As if reading her mind, Eddie kissed her temple in a gesture that strangely – unnervingly – reminded her of Bluey.

"Don't worry," Eddie said, "I'll take care of you."

"What about Wilkes?" Jack said to him.

Eddie shrugged. "If he's got any sense, he would've ridden out of there by now."

Wilkes? That must be the name of the rider who had—

A loud hoot made them all jump. About fifty feet upriver on the opposite bank hopped Mama, excitedly pointing, calling back over her shoulder. For Bluey, Pearl realised in shock. *I've found her*, Mama would be yelling. *Son, I've found your pet!* An eerie sense of inevitability froze Pearl's blood. No matter what she did, no matter where she fled or how far she ran, her destiny remained the same: to die in Bluey's paw. She knew this to be true.

Eddie and Jack, spurred into action, hauled Pearl upright. Her legs were nerveless. She hadn't the strength to stand. They lifted her by both arms and started to run. To where? *To where?* Pearl sobbed in helpless defeat. Meanwhile, Mama kept calling. A thrashing noise through the forest meant that Bluey was racing towards the river.

"No, please, I can't go any further," Pearl said. "Leave me here."

"Never," Eddie snarled through teeth, and the wild determination in his eyes cowed her.

Jack cried, "Get in the water!"

They dragged her to the bank and, in their haste, slipped in the mud and fell. The chill river closed over her head. Now she would drown. The murmur of the underwater tide sounded like a constant wind soughing about eaves. She opened her eyes. A clutch of yabbies, startled, flattened their segmented bodies into the riverbed and waved their pincers.

She was wrenched up by her arms. The water broke. Cold air gusted against her face.

"I'm the better swimmer, I'll take her," Jack said. "Turn onto your back, Eddie, and float. No, your *back*. It'll save your strength. Look around every now and again to check for rocks."

Jack's strong, wiry arm encircled her chest. She felt herself being pulled supine against his body. The current was carrying them away like it was carrying the dead leaves that hurried alongside. Like it had carried the corpse of Mutton Chop. Had the giant corpse snagged on a rock downstream? Would they bump into it? Or had it already sunk to the bottom with fish, eels, crabs and yabbies feasting on its decomposing flesh? The awful thought nauseated her. Distraught, she remembered Dot and lifted her head. Where was her little darling? Oh God, she couldn't see Dot—

But she could see Bluey.

He was at the bank, staring after her, his expression tense and frightened. To Bluey, it must seem that Pearl was being stolen. Kidnapped. What would he do? Could Yahoo-Devil-Devils even swim? She had no idea. But she was about to find out.

Bluey strode down the bank and waded in. Mama caterwauled and snatched at him. Undeterred, he took more strides towards mid-river until the water reached his chest. The current must have tugged at his heels and tripped him, because he fell back and thrashed in the water for a few seconds while Mama screamed. Lips pulling back over his teeth, lunging, he grabbed for the bank. Missed it. Grabbed again and held on. Safe. Mama put both arms about him and chittered. He didn't seem to notice. Mournful, he had eyes only for Pearl.

Pearl and Bluey stared at each other, never once breaking contact.

Then the river took a bend and Bluey was lost from sight.

10.

Early afternoon. Mrs Reginald Smith had wasted hours on supplication for nought. Riding upon her pony, Sugar, Mrs Smith headed along the dirt road towards home. George, astride his horse Belle, followed at a discreet distance. Good. Because Mrs Smith, weary and aggrieved, couldn't stop wiping tears from her eyes and she wanted privacy. Reginald must be dead. Lord Almighty. *She was a widow.* The realisation kept hitting her in fresh, agonising waves. How would she live without him? Cope without him?

And not just as a wife. How might Edna Smith continue running their sheep station when she had no understanding of its economics?

She hadn't a clue. About *any* of it.

Reginald had kept the books, dealt with staff and equipment maintenance, figured the worth of fleece, liaised with buyers and sellers and banks. Edna's concerns focused on running the household, managing the garden, laundry, caring for the dogs and horses, tending to any of the workers' minor medical issues that didn't require a doctor's expertise...

Edna thumbed at her eyes. Thankfully, George still maintained a respectful distance. She didn't want him to see her like this. Didn't want to reveal her weakness to him. To anybody. If she was to save this station, she'd need a brave front for as long as it took to figure things out.

Sugar, clopping a slow four-beat gait, turned from habit into the Smiths' driveway without Edna touching the reins. Their land lay flat. In the distance sat the long, single-storey house. The sight of it brought new tears. Without her husband, such a home was too big for Edna. They had no children. From cruel circumstance, however, not from choice. On their wedding day, they had looked forward to the joy of a large family. She had even picked out her favourite names for their brood-to-be: Arthur, Frederick, Ernest; Gladys, Vera, Thelma.

Well, what of it? No use picking at old scabs.

The future was her immediate concern.

Perhaps she could sell, return to Sydney. Why not? Her parents were still alive. They would shelter her until she got her bearings. She could re-enter society with enough coin to pivot into another well-paying industry. Perhaps a restaurant or nightclub. Even a medical clinic or school if she felt particularly philanthropic…

The beloved sights of the house, stables, pens and fences wrenched at her heart.

How could she leave?

The best years of her life had been lived at this station. How many lambs had she helped deliver? How many fruit trees and vegetables had she planted? How many meals had she made in the kitchen, her favourite room of the house? How many workers and their families befriended? How many evenings spent with Reginald catching up on the events of their respective days over their customary after-dinner glasses of port? Edna felt sick and dejected, lost and empty. Sugar's hooves tapped along the compacted earth of the driveway. The beloved homestead grew nearer. Edna whimpered at everything that it had ever meant to her.

"Mrs Smith?" George called. "Are you okay?"

"I'm perfectly fine. Please stay back."

Almost home. She could see the veranda and front door. Once inside, she would make a pot of tea and drink it on the patio in the back yard. The aromatic fragrances of the herb garden never failed to calm her. She would cut a slab of pound cake and eat every crumb.

Behind the homestead, a dust storm rose up from the mountainside as if a thin tornado had decided to cleave a path from top to bottom. Australia's outback embraced most kinds of weather events, but this one was new to Edna. She narrowed her eyes. Then she heard the noises: branches breaking, leaves thrashing, the frightened squawks of fleeing parrots. She tugged the reins to halt Sugar. The dust cloud got closer. Edna's heart knocked in her throat.

Could she be wrong?

Belle started to nicker and squeal.

"Whoa there, Belle," George was saying. "What's the matter, girl? Whoa there."

Two Yahoo-Devil-Devils burst from the bush and galloped across the property on their knuckles, slavering mouths open to reveal long and sharp teeth.

Sugar squealed, baulked, stuttered on her front feet and almost collapsed in fright.

The Yahoo-Devil-Devils smashed their fists across the house, pulverising the roof, strewing rafts of shattered shingles in every direction. Sheep bleated in terror. Young stable boys sprinted from the buildings. Edna screamed, loud and long, and the beasts spotted her.

Ran at her.

"George, get your gun!" Edna shouted, glancing behind.

But George was already whipping Belle in the opposite direction and disappearing at a rate of knots. Edna pulled Sugar's reins to turn around and flee. Sugar was too panicked to obey, shuffling and scrabbling her hooves in the dirt.

They were lifted off their feet. The sensation reminded Edna of her first date as a young girl with Reginald Smith. At a fairground, the seat of a Ferris wheel had gently touched the backs of their knees and knocked them both into a carriage to rise up, up, up, the land dropping away beneath them, the sky shining bright and clear.

***

Sodden from the river, weak and sore, limping on the soles of her torn feet, Pearl shuffled down Main Street. When she had fled from home less than a week ago, joining the boxing troupe with only a sunhat and suitcase, she could never have imagined – not in a million years – coming back so soon. Failure tasted bitter.

She cradled Dot in one arm. The poor darling was exhausted from the river journey, and slept against Pearl's breast. Eddie and Jack flanked Pearl, and Hopper brought up the rear. Men steered their horses and carts from the strange menagerie. Pedestrians stopped, gaped, recoiled. Parents turned their children away. Women hissed behind their hands about Pearl's nakedness. But she wore Eddie's shirt, didn't she? At any moment, Pearl expected to see the hostile, disapproving glare of her mother. It wouldn't be long. Someone who knew Mum would no doubt advise that the errant daughter had returned. Please God, Mum's boyfriend wouldn't see her first. At least Eddie held Pearl's hand. Oh, what a sight they all must make; so bruised and bloodied, dressed in little more than rags, Eddie bare-chested.

"Where's the police station?" Jack said.

"Up ahead on the left," Pearl said.

They planned to tell the sergeant of the dead. She remembered Big Stanley, Mr Smith, his worker unfolding like a pamphlet, the two riders. And Mavis... Gruff on the outside but kind and gentle, compassionate. Mavis had given Pearl one of her own blankets and fashioned a pillow for her out of sawdust. *If any of the punters gives you shit, I'll sort 'em out.*

A man came up to them. "You're badly injured, friends. A farm accident? Let me help."

"Much appreciated," Eddie said.

"After we give statements to the police," Jack said, "we'll need all the help you can offer. Thanks, mate. We've had a pretty rough trot—"

"Miss Pearl Bennett?" the man said, eyebrows lifting. "Is that you? Heavens above!"

Pearl took a closer look. It was the grocer, Mr Buchanan. Mum had run up quite a bill on credit. Mr Buchanan had threatened to box Pearl's ears if she didn't show up with the money.

"Yes, it's me," she sighed, "and I still can't pay."

"Your mother told us you'd eloped with a lawyer from Brisbane."

"Oh, did she? How silly of her to lie again." Pearl gave a wan smile. "Mr Buchanan, surely you recognise me from the boxing tent? It's well known that you like a flutter."

Reddening, he looked her up and down. "I'm a good Christian. My offer to help stands. But I'll have you know, Miss Bennett, I'll add the charges of food and water to your tab."

"Gee, you're all heart," Jack sneered. "Would you move? You're in our way."

Mr Buchanan, tsking, stepped aside and remarked to the nearest pedestrian, "That's Minnie Bennett's girl. My word. The state of her! Like mother like daughter, I always say."

"Yes, most assuredly, the apple never falls far from the tree," the elderly man said.

Squeezing Eddie's palm, fresh tears brimming, Pearl whispered, "God, I hate this town."

"Don't worry," he replied. "You won't be here long."

An older couple marched up to them, mouths cinched, nostrils flaring. The woman wore an expensive dress with a bodice that crammed her fat towards her neck. The man was kitted out like a dandy in a cutaway frock coat. Recognition made Pearl stiffen in shock. Why, it was Florence and Gilbert, the owners of Taylor's Travelling Troupe! They looked fresh and powdered, well rested, sated from a leisurely lunch of wine and roasted meat.

Jack began, "Boss, there's some awful bad news we've got to—"

"Rogues!" Florence chided. "Where's that car you stole?"

"We're taking the vehicle's full cost out of your wages," Gilbert said. "You're lucky we don't march the lot of you straight to the police station and demand your immediate arrest."

"There's no time for that now," Florence said. "Tell them, dear."

"If we're to make the next booking, you'll have to chop-chop, quick smart. The tent's back at the sheep station. I'll hire us a coach—"

"At *your* expense, mind, not ours, I'm keeping a tally—"

"And we'll set up with only two days lost," Gilbert went on. "Good thing you brought back Hopper. But you'll work double-time for nothing until we tell you the debt is cleared."

"Ugh, the *state* of you louts!" Florence scolded. "And *you*, you stupid girl. Good gracious, how Big Stanley convinced me to hire you, I'll never know. What are we supposed to do without Bluey? Our main attraction! Perhaps he was getting too big anyway, but that's not the point. Now we'll have to try and catch another one. Until we can, you'll not only be our cook and cleaner but my personal maid too, without any wage, not even a tuppence. You'd better be grateful for the meals you'll eat at my expense or out you go, straight on your ear."

"And where's Big Stanley and Mavis the Mauler?" Gilbert said, craning his neck as if the dead boxers were straggling somewhere behind. "And Tom, for that matter, the blasted lazy so-and-so. We paid that lousy mick a week in advance—"

Jack extended an arm to gently pop Gilbert Taylor in the face. Gilbert staggered back with a bloodied nose. Affronted, Florence gasped, pressing a hand against her prodigious bust.

"How dare you," she said. "You utter savage. Right, we're turning to the law."

"Oh, please just fuck off," Pearl advised.

Jack threw back his head and laughed.

Eddie grinned at Pearl. "How very nicely put, my darling."

"Why, thank you, honey. And to think, I've never spoken that word before in all my life."

Florence swept away, the frills of her dress flouncing. Gilbert tottered after her in jelly-legged pursuit. Pearl giggled. Then the church bell started to ring in a clanging, non-stop, concussive resonance, which clenched Pearl's gut. Townsfolk froze in anxiety. A few looked around, sudden fear etched on their faces. Others began to run. The odd shriek broke out.

"What's going on?" Jack said.

"Danger," Pearl said. "The bell's rhythm means 'seek shelter'. Usually from bushfire."

Collectively, they turned their heads towards the mountains. No flames. But there was a dust trail whipping closer. Instinctively, Pearl, Eddie and Jack huddled against one another. They each knew what the dust trail meant, even if the townsfolk didn't. Not yet.

The people on Main Street scattered. Some ran in circles, bamboozled by indecision. Those that fled were no doubt returning home to pack their essential belongings and race away by horse, or to retreat into basements and hope for the best. The volunteers of the fire brigade might head towards the dams and prime their pumps, or they might run. But this wasn't a bushfire. Pearl felt her knees buckle. Eddie and Jack stopped her from falling.

"Where should we go?" Jack said.

"The police station," Eddie said. "They'll have guns and ammo."

Fitting a hand each beneath her armpits, they lifted Pearl and ran with her. Dot woke up. Snuffling and sniffing, the terrier licked at Pearl's chin and whined, as if feeling the tension that gripped them and the whole town. Dot jumped from her arms and ran. Hopper kept pace. The furious church bell rang on and on and on.

Pearl's mind reeled. Just last night – only last night, which felt so very long ago! – Eddie had sprung Pearl feeding apples to Bluey. On a whim, she had hauled off the cage cover…

I want him to see his home again. Surely, you can't begrudge a small kindness.

How are we supposed to put the covering back on without the hooks and pulleys?

Her actions had doomed them all. Every death so far, and every death still to come, was on her own contemptible head. It was enough to make her swoon.

Sudden movement above the rooftops of Main Street caught her eye. Silver, brandishing a severed tree trunk, his face disfigured by wrath. Pearl's fear locked the scream in her throat. Eddie and Jack, unaware, kept running.

Silver swung the trunk at the highest building, the two-storey town hall, and smashed off the clock tower. The sound was explosive. Flying bricks slammed into the street. Shop windows smashed. Townsfolk screamed and fled. A few were struck down. Horses reared and bolted, shrieking. The church bell rang continuously.

One-Eye loped across the square, grabbed hold of the belltower and wrenched it loose with the ease of plucking a flower. The rhythmic ringing stopped. Shingles and stone blocks showered over Main Street. Men and women were hit. A perambulator crumpled. In One-Eye's hands, the clapper banged about at random until he tugged the bell free from its rope and bit at its sound bow, shutting the bell's mouth like closing a book. He threw the bell and it tumbled, hitting the pub, barrelling through the bricks with the power of a cannonball. Undermined, the front wall of the pub teetered and got ready to fall.

You can't escape Fate, Pearl thought dizzily. Whatever Fate has planned, that's it—

"Come on!" Eddie shouted, hauling her through an open door.

A barber's shop.

Cowering, wailing, staff and customers hid in the back. Resisting Eddie's pull, Pearl raced to the window. The rest of the Yahoo-Devil-Devil clan burst through the town – breaking and pounding, ruining every structure – including the females, which didn't make sense. Shouldn't Mama and Farthing be ensconced in their bolthole, letting their males fight the battle? And yet here they were, both females vengeful, each holding their child in one arm and, with the other, picking up abandoned carts to smash underfoot. The screech of tethered and wounded cart-horses sounded eerily like panicked women.

Bluey walked into Main Street.

Pearl's heart leapt. Yet Bluey was round-shouldered, defeated. Ambling like he didn't care. She remembered the clear weep from his gunshot wound. Oh, might he be dying…?

"Get away," Eddie said, dragging Pearl from the window. "It's too dangerous."

Pearl threw off his grip and pressed her face against the glass.

What a gruesome sight! Every able-bodied person had deserted Main Street. Now, only the dead and injured littered the road and footpaths. She heard groans and cries for help. Dear God… But the Yahoo-Devil-Devil clan had paused. Why? Had their thirst for carnage been quenched already? They gathered in a loose circle. Farthing approached the centre of the circle and laid something gently, tenderly, onto the dirt. What was it?

Pearl rubbed away tears, and looked again. Couldn't believe the sight.

Bubs.

The something that Farthing had laid down on the dirt was Bubs. Limp, his blue eyes open, staring blindly at the infinite. Bubs! Dead and stilled forever. Stunned, Pearl recalled Wilkes' shot. *Farthing shrieked and fell back. Was she wounded? Or just startled?* Wilkes had aimed at Farthing but had hit her baby.

In a paroxysm of renewed ferocity, the Yahoo-Devil-Devils pulled at buildings and brought them down. Bricks, tiles and shingles tumbled. Screams sounded. *Human* screams. Pearl started in awful realisation. The townsfolk hadn't retreated to their homes and basements: without time to flee, they had hidden inside shops like Pearl, Eddie and Jack—

Gripping her wrist, Eddie said, "Step back from the window, Pearl. You might get cut."

"But they're going to kill everyone!"

"We can't help that."

Farthing began to wail. A single note; a mournful cry. The other Yahoo-Devil-Devils howled in sympathy and beat at their chests – *thock thock thock* – in a clear and increasingly aggressive proclamation. The total destruction of the town was about to commence.

Pearl brushed off Eddie's grasp, opened the door and limped outside.

"Stop!" Eddie called. "Pearl, come back!"

She was the only ambulant human in Main Street. Corpses lay in broken disarray. The injured crawled, moaned, rocked back and forth in agony. Wounded horses shrilled. Barefoot, Pearl picked her way over smashed tiles and bricks. Momentarily, she wanted to turn back and hide, but no, no... The cloak of Fate had settled fast about her shoulders, prickling and needling, inevitable.

"Bluey!" she called. "Bluey!"

He sat spraddle-legged in the street. Mama had both arms about his neck.

Bluey coughed out a single bark. The other Yahoo-Devil-Devils stopped their chest-thumping and battle-crying to watch Pearl's approach. She staggered towards Bubs.

Yes, the poor little one was dead, shot through the head.

Tears rose.

Bubs looked at Pearl, his enormous blue eyes fringed with dark lashes, and smiled. Why, he had only four blunt teeth; two on the top and two on the bottom, like a human infant...

Silver and One-Eye snarled. They hovered with their hands clawed as if to rip Pearl to shreds. Bluey flung out his arm, which stopped them.

Mama hugged Bluey closer. Did Mama have tears in her eyes too?

Regardless, heedless, mindless, Pearl advanced. Wilkes' shot had penetrated Bubs' temple, visible by a spot of dried blood. Pearl fell to her knees and stroked the strawberry-blonde head already cold, touched the face already setting in death, and began to cry. Dear Bubs. He'd been fascinated with Dot and had treated the terrier with reverence. Where was Dot? Pearl didn't know. She sobbed openly, loudly, hugging Bubs' corpse, wishing that life's random cruelty had thrown a different set of dice. Something touched her. Pearl looked up. Bluey was stroking at her back with a gentle forefinger.

"I'm so sorry," Pearl whispered. "Oh, really I am."

"Me too," Eddie said.

Startled, Pearl turned her head. Eddie was right next to her, patting Bubs' fur. The Yahoo-Devil-Devils watched them quietly, curiously, moving closer to get a better view. Then Jack hobbled over, knelt next to Pearl and Eddie, and laid his palm on Bubs' arm.

"Aw, bloody hell," he muttered through his broken jaw. "Everything about this is shitty."

Bluey's face looked stricken and pained. The bullet hole in his shoulder oozed a thick, yellow and deadly discharge. He reached out for Pearl. She didn't resist or try to flee. Instead, she allowed Bluey to gather her into his paw. So be it. She smiled as he lifted her. He grinned back with moist eyes. Pearl stroked his thumb.

"I'm ready," she said. "Let's go."

"Go where?" Eddie said. "No. Where are you going? What are you doing?"

With difficulty, Bluey stood up, holding Pearl.

"Bye, Eddie," she whispered. "Look after him, Jack."

"Will do."

"No, you don't have to do this." Panting, haggard, Eddie dragged himself to his feet. "Bluey, stop. Put her down or I'll shoot." He hauled the revolver from his waistband and click-click-clicked the empty barrel. Staggering a little, he patted himself down for bullets.

Bluey started to shuffle away, cradling Pearl. The Yahoo-Devil-Devils followed; their collective anger spent. Bubs' corpse got left behind for reasons unknown.

"Pearl!" Eddie called. "*Pearl!*"

The anguish in his voice brought fresh tears to her eyes.

The Yahoo-Devil-Devils walked from Main Street, heading west. The occasional gunshot sounded. A few townsfolk were fighting back. Too late. The battle had ended. As the clan marched towards the ranges, Eddie's plaintive calls got fainter until they disappeared.

After a time, the clan reached the Smiths' station. Pearl saw the destroyed homestead, the bloodied corpses of men and sheep, the ruined tent of Taylor's Travelling Troupe, and hid her face in her hands. The clan stepped over the back fence and tramped into the forest.

The greenery smelled clean, fresh, like mint and lemon. Climbing the mountain, the Yahoo-Devil-Devils pushed through branches. Pearl had seen this ascent before, yet in a dream: snoozing in the carriage of a rickety, rocking old train that rattled along tracks and jostled her, the memory provoking visions of Grandma…

Pearl felt sick.

A deep, hot illness was shooting through her. An infection from one of her many cuts?

Oh, what difference did it make?

Clutching at Bluey's paw, Pearl wept as she let herself imagine what life might have been like if she'd been able to share it with Eddie. Perhaps a wedding, a cottage, finding strength in each other's love, having babies and watching their children grow, weathering the storms of existence as man and wife, growing old together. All of that future lost. All of it gone.

Bluey kissed Pearl's crown. He stank of rotten eggs and spoiled fish. The clan began to hum and sing. Following along, Bluey stomped further into the greenery, heading up and up.

He would forget to give Pearl water. Offer her nothing but leaves to eat.

Colourful lorikeets, squawking, darted and drew her attention. Pearl gazed about and wondered what dying might be like out here in the Australian outback. Not so bad. As exhausted as she was, death no longer seemed to matter that much anymore.

END

Check out other great

Cryptid Novels!

J.H. Moncrieff

RETURN TO DYATLOV PASS

In 1959, nine Russian students set off on a skiing expedition in the Ural Mountains. Their mutilated bodies were discovered weeks later. Their bizarre and unexplained deaths are one of the most enduring true mysteries of our time. Nearly sixty years later, podcast host Nat McPherson ventures into the same mountains with her team, determined to finally solve the mystery of the Dyatlov Pass incident. Her plans are thwarted on the first night, when two trackers from her group are brutally slaughtered. The team's guide, a superstitious man from a neighboring village, blames the killings on yetis, but no one believes him. As members of Nat's team die one by one, she must figure out if there's a murderer in their midst—or something even worse—before history repeats itself and her group becomes another casualty of the infamous Dead Mountain.

Gerry Griffiths

CRYPTID ZOO

As a child, rare and unusual animals, especially cryptid creatures, always fascinated Carter Wilde. Now that he's an eccentric billionaire and runs the largest conglomerate of high-tech companies all over the world, he can finally achieve his wildest dream of building the most incredible theme park ever conceived on the planet... CRYPTID ZOO. Even though there have been apparent problems with the project, Wilde still decides to send some of his marketing employees and their families on a forced vacation to assess the theme park in preparation for Opening Day. Nick Wells and his family are some of those chosen and are about to embark on what will become the most terror-filled weekend of their lives—praying they survive. STEP RIGHT UP AND GET YOUR FREE PASS... TO CRYPTID ZOO

www.ingramcontent.com/pod-product-compliance
Lightning Source LLC
Chambersburg PA
CBHW072238190626
46809CB00018B/2838
9781922551030